## About the Author

The author has studied philosophy in undergraduate school and English Literature in graduate school. He has a good sense of humor, though sometimes he has trouble transmitting that into his fiction.

# The Soaring Hawk

Paul Devito

# The Soaring Hawk

Olympia Publishers
*London*

www.olympiapublishers.com
OLYMPIA PAPERBACK EDITION

Copyright © Paul Devito 2023

The right of Paul Devito to be identified as author of
this work has been asserted in accordance with sections 77 and 78 of
the Copyright, Designs and Patents Act 1988.

**All Rights Reserved**

No reproduction, copy or transmission of this publication
may be made without written permission.
No paragraph of this publication may be reproduced,
copied or transmitted save with the written permission of the publisher,
or in accordance with the provisions
of the Copyright Act 1956 (as amended).

Any person who commits any unauthorized act in relation to
this publication may be liable to criminal
prosecution and civil claims for damage.

A CIP catalogue record for this title is
available from the British Library.

ISBN: 978-1-80439-365-9

This is a work of fiction.
Names, characters, places and incidents originate from the writer's
imagination. Any resemblance to actual persons, living or dead, is
purely coincidental.

First Published in 2023

Olympia Publishers
Tallis House
2 Tallis Street
London
EC4Y 0AB

Printed in Great Britain

# Dedication

I dedicate this book to Tami Rodriguez

# Acknowledgments

I thank everyone in my family for their support.

# Chapter One

I was walking on the beach alone, looking out over the great expanse of the ocean, thinking about Linda and planning our life together. I looked behind me and watched my footprints melt away like the past. I was starting a new life, clean and sober, and engaged to a beautiful young woman.

She was back at the hotel getting ready for dinner. Our lovemaking had been intense, and the memory of it was vivid. After a while, I walked back to the halfway house and saw George and Eliot.

"You seem like you're in a better mood," Eliot said.

"She agreed to marry me," I said with a big smile.

"How did you manage to convince her?"

"We were making love, and I pressured here into it," I said, laughing.

"I hope she doesn't change her mind," George said.

"She won't," I said with little confidence.

"Is she good in bed?" Eliot asked.

"Yeah, she's great."

"Well, you'd better give Laura the news," George said.

"I hadn't thought about that."

"She's young; she'll get over it," George said.

"I hate to hurt her feelings."

"She already knows about Linda. She's not going to be hurt," George said.

I decided to call Linda, to see if she was ready to go out.

"Hey, what's up?" I said.

"I'm ready," she said.

"How do you feel?"

"Great! How about you?"

"I feel good too."

"Where are we going tonight?"

"There's a small seafood place not too far away. You'll like it."

"Oh, what time are you going to pick me up?"

"I'll be there in half an hour."

After I hung up, I jumped in the shower and dressed quickly. George lent me his car, and I was excited to see my new fiancé. When I arrived at her door, I was greeted by the most beautiful girl I had ever seen. Linda had gone all out. Part of her blonde hair was pulled back, and she had strands hanging by the side of her face. She was wearing a short black dress that was low-cut, and had pearls around her neck. Her face was lightly tanned; all I could think about was fucking her right there.

"Wow!" I exclaimed.

"You like?" she smiled.

"You look great!"

"How do you like the dress?"

"It's fantastic."

I kissed her and whispered into her ear that I wanted to fuck her.

"Not now. We're going to dinner; I'm starved."

"You win."

We walked out into the evening light, which was a deep orange. I loved California, especially in the morning and at dusk when the light was so beautiful. We got into the old Mercedes and drove along the coast.

"Can we really afford to live here?" she asked.

"I think so. We're not going to be able to live right on the beach or anything, but we can get pretty close."

"I think my parents would be a little upset that I was living so far away, but they'll get used to the idea. As long as we have each other, it'll feel like home."

"I was thinking earlier," I said, "we didn't really set a time schedule for our marriage."

"I thought maybe we should live together for a year," she said.

"That's all right with me."

As we drove along the beach, I opened the windows and let the warm wind pass through my hair. I couldn't remember the last time I felt so happy. I gazed out over the ocean and wished this moment would last forever. When we arrived at the restaurant, we noticed there were a lot of people there. It was a popular spot.

"Do you feel like waiting in line for a while, or do you want to go someplace else?" I asked.

"Let's just wait; the food must be good."

"All right."

We sat among quite a few people; they said it would be a half-hour wait. After a few minutes, I got antsy and said I wanted to get out of there. I wasn't comfortable in a crowd, and I was hungry.

"Where do you want to go?" Linda said.

"I know of another place, and their food is just as good."

We got back into the car and drove back along the coast.

"When did you know that you wanted to marry me?" she asked.

"I guess I've always had it in my mind, but just recently the feeling got a lot stronger."

"Why recently?"

"What do you mean?"

"I'm just feeling a little pressured is all. You came to rehab, and now you seem like a different person."

My heart leaped into my throat. I could tell she was trying to back out of our commitment.

"Actually, I'm feeling more like myself than I have in several years."

"I have to get used to this new you," she said.

"I'm not that different; quit exaggerating. Do you still love me?" I asked.

"Of course, yes, but I think we should hold off on this marriage stuff."

"Well, we decided to live together for a year; that should be sufficient time."

"I don't want to hurt your feelings, but I think we should go back to Syracuse."

I didn't say anything for a long time. We arrived at the other restaurant, and we were seated immediately. I wanted to order a drink in the worst way, but didn't. I was feeling angry, sad, and frustrated. I was thinking she was too young to be serious about marriage. She was only twenty-one and didn't have much experience. I, on the other hand, was ready to settle down and wanted desperately to get out of the dating scene.

"Are you sure you don't want to live in California?" I asked.

"I'm not sure of anything right now," she replied.

"I don't understand," I said.

"Please don't get angry."

"I'm just frustrated is all. This afternoon you said you would marry me, and now you're not sure of anything."

Our food came pretty quickly. We both ate steak, and it was good, but I couldn't enjoy it, and I don't think she did either. I could hear Eliot's voice in my mind telling me to back off and let her be.

"Listen, if you need more time to think about it, that's fine," I said. "We'll go back to Syracuse and live separately. That way there won't be any pressure."

"You're great," she said. "Thanks for being so understanding."

We left the restaurant, after eating mostly in silence. I was still upset, but at least a decision had been made. I hadn't thought of it earlier, but perhaps she wanted to see if I could stay clean and sober. I was more determined than ever to clean up my act, and she was responsible for a lot of it.

# Chapter Two

I thought she might want to have sex that night, but she didn't. I went back to the halfway house and talked with Eliot. He basically listened as I poured my heart out, but as usual, he was optimistic.

"Of course, she's young, but if you play your cards right, you can stay with her," he said.

"I have a lot of fear, and no confidence," I said.

"You need to distance yourself a bit, and go through family therapy as you planned."

We sat up talking until late at night, and I went to bed exhausted. I had trouble sleeping and tossed and turned all night. In the morning, I got up early and went for a long walk on the beach. The water was calm, and the sun was just rising. It was beautiful. When I got back to the house, George was showering, and Eliot was making cappuccino.

"You're up early as usual," Eliot said.

"I couldn't sleep last night. I probably only got two hours."

"You need to get some real exercise and tire out your body," he said.

"Should I call Linda?"

"Let her sleep."

"I guess I'll let her call me; she's got a lot of thinking to do."

"Good idea. Don't pressure her."

We sat in the kitchen, the morning light coming brightly through the window. I was thinking that in the old days, I would be rolling a joint and kicking back. Now there was more stress, reality was hitting like a ton of bricks, and there was no escaping.

"What are you doing today?" I asked Eliot.

"George and I are going to the beach. Do you want to go?"

"Yeah, I think I will. It might be a good idea to leave Linda alone today. I'll call her later."

"How's that latte?" he asked.

"Good. We should own a Starbucks or something."

"What are you going to do, Paul, stay here or go back to Syracuse?"

"I don't know yet. Linda wants to go back to Syracuse, but I'm still undecided. I have yet to let a woman make a decision for me, and I don't think I'm going to now."

"You should stay out here; she'll stay if she wants to."

George got out of the shower, and I decided to take one. It was tempting to stay in California and start my life over again. There were plenty of women, and I loved the beauty of the beach. I didn't think I could give up Linda, though; she was the best woman I had ever been with. I wondered if she might transfer to a school out here where we could be close together.

After I took my shower, the three of us went to the beach. It was a warm day, and it was enjoyable first to be there and talk.

"You need a girlfriend, Eliot," I said.

"Jennifer will do for now," he said.

"I think I'm a love addict," I said.

"No, you're a sex addict," George said.

"Sex and love then," I said, laughing.

"If Linda didn't want to have sex, would you still be with her?" George asked.

"What kind of a question is that?" I said.

"Seriously," he said.

"No, I don't think I would be, but maybe in twenty years I would," I said.

"You just lust after her," he said.

"No, I don't."

"He likes her, but I don't think he knows the responsibility of being in love," Eliot said.

"You guys are jealous," I said.

"I'm not," George said. "I have a wife who loves me and five children."

"I'm a little jealous," Eliot said.

I looked out over the ocean to the islands offshore. The water was calm, and the atmosphere helped me relax. A while later, we walked over to the hot dog stand and got something to eat.

"You'd better give her a call," Eliot said. "She'll be worried about you, and she doesn't have anything to do."

"You're right," I said.

There was a payphone not too far away, and I went to call her.

"Hi, sweetheart," I said.

"What have you been doing all morning?" she said.

"We've been at the beach. Do you want to join us?"

"Of course; come and pick me up."

I drove to get her in the old blue Mercedes, and was pleasantly surprised to see her in a slinky white bikini.

"Hey, you look great," I said.

"I want to apologize," she said. "I'm a bit confused right now, and I said some things that I'm not sure I meant."

"Don't worry about it. I'm confused too," I said.

"I think I do want to marry you."

"Let's give it some time. I'm going through a lot right now, and I want to concentrate on staying sober."

"See, that's something I know nothing about. I think I can help you, but I don't know what to do."

"Just encourage me to go to my support group meetings and to stay away from friends who smoke pot."

"I can do that."

We drove the few blocks to the beach and hooked up with George and Eliot. I wanted to fuck her so bad, and I was thinking that I would get some that evening. We sat together facing the ocean, and I felt so peaceful that afternoon. I imagined walking down the aisle with her and having a couple of kids.

"You look hot," Eliot said to Linda.

"So do you," Linda said.

"Hey, no flirting," I said.

"I thought I would cook tonight," George said.

"Good idea. What are you cooking?" Eliot said.

"Well, the only thing I know how to cook is steak, which limits our options a bit."

"I love steak," Linda said.

"Eliot will help me cook, and you two can clean up," George said.

We spent several more hours at the beach, and it was perfectly enjoyable to stretch out and relax. I fell asleep for a while listening to the gentle breeze and the seagulls. Most of the time, I was staring at Linda's legs and her delicious ass. At about five, we went back to the house and George started cooking. We made instant mashed potatoes and steamed some broccoli, along with the steak.

"So, are you guys getting married or what?" George said during dinner.

"We're going to wait a while," I said.

"I think it's best if we go back to Syracuse as I can finish my studies," Linda said.

"I might stay here," I said.

Linda looked at me in disbelief.

"You might stay here?" she said.

"I was thinking about it."

"You didn't tell me that. I thought it was decided."

"Nothing is decided."

She got very angry and stormed out of the room. She left the house and walked back to the hotel. The guys didn't say anything, and I pretended I was playing it cool. I was angry as well and frustrated. Seriously, I was thinking of staying in California and letting her go back by herself. I liked California, and it felt like a new life for me. The sunshine would help me paint, and I would be even freer out here. Finally, George spoke up.

"You don't have to decide right now; she's going to fly back in a few days, and you're going to be here for a few more months."

"I've never been good at tying my life to somebody else."

"Me neither," Eliot said.

"She'll get over her anger, and she has a lot of thinking to do," George said.

I wanted to be back in my apartment, painting, with a little peace of mind. They said one should not be in a relationship the first year of recovery, and now I know why. I loved her, but I had a lot of trouble handling my emotions. *If we had been in Syracuse, we wouldn't have gone through this,* I thought.

# Chapter Three

I took extra medication that night, to be sure of sleeping, and it worked. I got up early, feeling refreshed. I walked along the beach, before the sun was up, and listened to the birds. The moon was a sliver in the sky, with a ring around it. There was no more peaceful time of day. When I got back to the house, George was showering, and Eliot was making coffee.

"How do you feel this morning?" Eliot asked.

"A lot better. I slept well."

"Good."

"What's going on today?" I asked.

"We're going to the junkyard to get some parts for the Mercedes."

"How's your truck running?"

"Decent, not great. I have to bring it into the shop," he said.

"I have to talk to Linda; it's only slightly ironic that one day we're getting married, then we're breaking up."

"You're not breaking up."

"It feels that way."

"Give her a call; you'll see she's cooled off by now."

"There are a few major things we haven't resolved yet, though."

I decided to wait another hour or so before I called her. I imagined she hadn't slept well, and I was right.

"Hi, honey," I said.

"Good morning. What time is it?" she said.

"It's seven. Usually, you're up by now. Do you want to go back to sleep?"

"Just for a little while. I tossed and turned all night," she said.

"All right; I'll call you later."

At least she hadn't sounded angry. I took a shower and shaved, thinking that perhaps today we would make love. I said goodbye to the guys; we made plans to get together for lunch. I waited another hour, then called Linda again.

"I'm up now," she said.

"I'm sorry about last night," I said. "I'm confused right now, is all."

"Well, you've confused me too," she said.

"I'll come pick you up in a few minutes; we have therapy today," I said.

I walked over to the hotel. The sun was shining as usual, and I felt pretty good. She was wearing a short white skirt and a small tank top. She looked great. We walked back to the house and waited until it was time for therapy. We walked over to the rehab and found our little room. Chairs were put in a circle, and there were some classical prints of Monet on the wall. There was a sliding glass door to the outside, and one could see many of the plants and flowers outside. It was a very relaxing setting.

"Let's get started," Janet the therapist said.

It was mostly family members, with their alcoholic adult children.

"Let's go around the room and say how we're feeling today," she said.

When they arrived at me, I said, "I feel in love, frustrated, angry, a little depressed, and happy!"

Everybody laughed, except Linda, who said she was frustrated. We listened to everybody else's problems and realized ours were small in comparison. Then it was Linda's turn to talk.

"I love Paul," she started, "but he is going through something now that I don't understand. He is changing every day, and he can't make a decision, which leaves me out in the cold."

"How do you feel about that, Paul?" Janet asked.

"I understand how she feels, but I can't see the changes in me. I feel like the same person I've always been."

Nothing was resolved, of course, but we felt better after leaving the meeting. We walked hand in hand back to the house and found the guys already there. Now I wanted to marry her and live happily ever after.

"Hey, what's up?" George said.

"We went to therapy; it seemed to help some," I said.

"Boy, some of these people have serious problems; ours were trivial in comparison," Linda said.

"Yeah, they create most of their problems," Eliot said. "Their minds are a mess."

"That's the one thing about Paul, which has always been consistent," Linda said. "He's a good thinker."

"All those years of studying," George said, "I wish I had that background."

"Maybe, but since I've got into recovery, my emotions have been a disaster, and that has clouded my thinking," I said.

"That must be the change in you," she said. "You were always so cool before."

"It's easy to be cool all the time when you're fucked up. It's a different thing in recovery," I said.

"I'll get used to you," she said.

That was the kindest comment she had made in two days. I was really struggling, and I needed her support. The guys were staying cool. I would have to draw off their strength. We made lunch. We were eating less often in the cafeteria; Eliot enjoyed cooking, and so did I sometimes, but we all took turns. We had some leftover chicken, which Eliot cut up and stir fried with some vegetables.

"Maybe I will come out here," Linda suddenly said. "That Syracuse weather is horrible."

"The schools are cheaper out here, once you establish residency," Eliot said.

"I know. That's what Paul was telling me."

"I hope you guys stay together," George said.

I looked at Linda, but she looked away. We really were in love, but it was at a difficult period in my life. I thought maybe in a year or two things would settle down, and all I would have to do is ride it out. The rest of the meal we ate in silence. I was thinking about the future. I was scared that Linda and I wouldn't be able to stay together.

After lunch, Linda and I lay down and took a nap. I rubbed her ass, and she rubbed my cock, but we didn't make love.

"I love you," I said.

"I love you too."

I had the most peaceful sleep I had had in a long time. I had a sweet dream, which I don't remember, and woke up feeling refreshed.

"What would you like to do?" I asked.

"I'd like to go to the beach again," she said.

"You're starting to like it out here."

"Yeah, perhaps I'll stay another week," she said.

"I have a better idea. Why don't you come out for the summer?"

"That sounds great."

"I don't want to fight any more, sweetheart. Let's try to get along, no matter what happens," I said.

"I don't like fighting either."

I kissed her, and the next thing you know, we were making love. She was so soft, and I touched her so tenderly. I loved licking her pussy, and she loved sucking my cock. I came quickly, but she wasn't disappointed. The next time, I told her, we would make love for hours.

We went to the beach and baked the bitterness out of our bodies. I wanted to be home, painting, with her naked in front of me, but that was not to be. I often had cravings for pot, but I had learned how to swiftly suppress them. She wanted to talk about her work at school, so we talked some theory.

"Are you a deconstructionist?" she asked me.

"Not really," I said. "There's a fundamental contradiction in their theory."

"Really, what's that?"

"Well, they're atheists, but they also claim to be skeptics; you can't have it both ways. If you know god doesn't exist, you can't claim not to know anything."

"But you're atheist. Why?"

"Because I know the extent and quality of evil. It's a classic argument. And since I claim to know that God doesn't exist, I can also claim to know that pure repetition is impossible. Here is where I agree with the deconstructionists. My interpretation of atheism will always be slightly different. It's between repetition and difference."

"You've lost me."

"Don't worry about it; we'll talk about it some other time."

We walked along the shore, gazing out over the expanse of the ocean. The water was clear and cold, and we walked for a long time. I wanted to bring up marriage again, but thought better of it. I was in no position to get married, and I didn't want to fail at it my first time.

"You're more like yourself today," she said.

"You have no idea what I'm going through," I said.

"I wish you hadn't smoked pot at all."

"So do I," I said. "Do you want to go swimming?"

"Are you crazy? It's too cold."

"In Sweden, they do."

"Well, we're not in Sweden."

"We can pretend we're in Sweden."

"I don't have a suit on anyway," she said.

"We can go naked," I suggested.

"There are people around."

"So, who cares?"

"I do," she said. "Quit kidding."

"Do you want to get a hot dog?"

"Sure."

"We walked over to the hot dog stand and ordered our food. I felt good that day, but it wasn't going to last; I knew that. Most days I felt good, but every few days I had a bad one.

"Do you like Eliot and George?" I asked her.

"Yeah, I think they're great; I'm glad I didn't meet them when they were using. George is really sweet. I can imagine him being married. I bet he's really good with his kids."

"Eliot's a great family man, too," I said, "but I haven't met his kids. They're grown up. Do you know he was captain of the fire department when he got arrested, and they plastered his picture on the front page of the newspaper? He did eight months in jail, then came here."

We walked a little more with our food, then went back to the house. Eliot was working on his paperwork for therapy, and

George was out.

"Did you guys make love on the beach?" Eliot said.

"This man wanted to go swimming in the nude!" Linda said.

"What's wrong with that?" Eliot asked, smiling.

"You guys are perverted!" she said, laughing.

"Only slightly," Eliot said.

## Chapter Four

George arrived a few minutes later. He had gone to Starbucks for a little break.

"Hey, what's up?" I said.

"I talked to my wife," he said. "We're getting back together."

"We knew that," Eliot said.

"Yeah, but the more often I hear it, the more I'm convinced."

Linda and I sat close together at the kitchen table, and I couldn't help think that we really made a great couple. I wished only that she were a little older. I felt better when I was around her, unless we were arguing. She had completely different beliefs than I, but it didn't matter as far as getting along was concerned.

"You're getting quite a tan there, girl," George said.

"My friends are going to be so jealous back in Syracuse," she said.

"Life is pretty good out here," Eliot said, looking at me.

"What are you going to do when you get out of here?" Linda asked Eliot.

"I'm going back to school to become a counselor; I've already signed up for classes."

"Maybe you could do that, Paul," she said. "You'd be a great counselor."

"I might. I also thought I would run for President of the United States."

"I would vote for you," George said.

"We could have scandalous parties in the White House,"

Eliot said.

"No more parties for me," I said.

"You can still have fun in recovery," Eliot said. "You just can't drink or smoke."

"Maybe I'll join Arthur Murray and take dance lessons," I said.

"We can still go dancing, can't we?" Linda said.

"Of course," I said.

It was nice to loosen up a little and not take my days so seriously. Linda had a great sense of humor, but you had to get her going.

"Why don't we dance now?" Eliot said.

He went into the living room and put in one of his old disco tapes. The house livened up, and we all started moving around. I laughed when Eliot grabbed Linda and spun her around. I spanked her ass and took her hands.

"You're a good dancer," she said.

"So are you."

After dancing for a while, we turned down the music and sat at the kitchen table.

"I burned a little today," Linda said.

"We don't go out in the sun much; we're so used to it," George said.

"Your wife has quite a tan though," Eliot said.

"Yeah, she's vain. What can I say?"

"And you're not?" Eliot said.

"We're all vain," Linda said.

We shot the breeze for a while and enjoyed ourselves as if we were somewhere else. Actually, I was surprised that Linda could put up with all this bullshit, but I wasn't going to question it too much. She loved me; perhaps if she had been older and wiser, she would have stayed away from me. It was getting to be dinner time, so we decided to barbecue, since there was one on the premises. We had some chicken and sausage, and Linda volunteered to make instant mashed potatoes. I felt relaxed, which was unusual at that period in my life.

"What do you guys do back in Syracuse? I know the winters are impossible," George said.

"I study all the time, but we have the university, which has lots of movies, and plays, and art shows."

"I got stoned," I said, laughing, but it was true unfortunately.

"You did a lot more than that," Linda said. "He has some really interesting old friends back there. They're all artists and musicians; they have a lot of fun."

"Yeah, we have fun, but things are going to change if I go back; I'm not hanging out with my old friends any more. They all smoke pot."

"Giving up your old friends is the most difficult part of recovery," Eliot said.

I thought about that carefully, which made me want to stay in California even more. I wanted a new start, but I also didn't think that I could leave Linda behind, so I was really torn. The past haunted me quite a bit; all I wanted to do was leave it behind. I knew it would take time to forget the past and establish a new sober history. Hopefully, Linda would be part of it.

"You play the keyboard a little, don't you, Paul?" Eliot said.

"Not very well, really; I'm much better at lip-synching. I can pretend to sing and play very well."

"You've got a lot of talent," George said.

"No, he's really pretty good," Linda said, "but his paintings are great."

"Stop, you're making me blush," I said with a laugh.

"I want him to teach me how to write fiction," she said. "You should read some of his poetry; it's beautiful."

"George doesn't read poetry," Eliot said.

"Like you do," George said.

"I've read a lot of poetry for your information," Eliot said. "I like the Romantics and Yeats."

"You surprise me every day, Eliot," I said. "I consider myself to be a Neo-Romantic."

Eliot had read some of my poetry. I had brought some with me, and I had written some there. It was much easier to write sober, and I was already planning my next novel. I couldn't motivate myself to paint, though, and I didn't know how I would do without the pot.

We ate, and the food was delicious. I enjoyed being sober. I was finally clear-headed, after years of being stoned. I was gaining weight in recovery; I had put on ten pounds since I had been in California. The exercise was helping, and smoking kept my eating down.

"Let's go out tonight," Linda said. "I want to go dancing."

"We can do that," I said, "but curfew is at eleven."

"We'll only go for a couple of hours," Eliot said.

"I'm in," George said, "and I know a good place where it's not too loud."

At nine, we went out, but we were just dressed casually. Linda was all excited, and was singing on the way to the club.

"Whatever you're on, girl, give some to me," George said, as he drove the Mercedes.

"A natural high is the best," she said.

When we arrived, the club was practically empty, but we didn't care. I felt uncomfortable the moment we walked in.

"I don't like this place," I said.

"You feel uncomfortable about the booze, don't you?" Eliot said.

"Yeah, let's get out of here," I said.

Linda had a disappointed look on her face, but she knew I was serious. We walked back out to the car and drove home. I apologized, but I suspected the other guys felt the same way. We put some music on at the house and took turns dancing with Linda.

"I'm sorry I couldn't stay at the club," I said to her as we danced.

"It's all right, I understand. I'd rather be here with you guys sober than be at the club with everyone drunk."

"That's a good way to look at it," I said.

A couple of hours later, I walked Linda back to the hotel. I went up with her and we made love. I had never felt so close to her as at that moment.

"I love you," I said.

"I love you too," she said.

I hustled back to the house and got back right before eleven. When I was in bed, I heard a knock on my window. It was Laura, and like a fool, I let her in.

"What are you doing here? We're going to get in trouble!"

"I missed you, and I'm jealous of your girlfriend. I want you back."

It was a warm evening, and all she was wearing was a tee shirt and panties. With her tan and long legs, she was irresistible.

"Come on in and shut the window."

She had a big smile on her face, and she practically tackled me.

"I think I'm in love with you," she said, laughing.

"Oh, stop, that's just rehab love; we've been through

something together, like a plane wreck, and you feel close to me; that's all."

"It's more than that," she said, as she took off her shirt.

I grabbed her and started sucking on her tits; she tasted so good. I pulled her panties off and tasted her juices. Then we fucked our brains out, but I didn't last as long as I wanted.

"How was that?" I said, exhausted.

"Great!"

"Now you'd better sneak back over to your house before somebody hears us."

After she left, I felt a little guilty, but I knew I was in love with Linda and thought it would never happen again. I slept well since I was so tired and woke up feeling refreshed. I got up before the guys and made myself a latte. It felt so good to be clean and sober; I was really feeling better, and I was starting to concentrate better.

After I drank my coffee, I went running, but only lasted a mile since I was so out of shape. The beach was beautiful in the morning, and I looked out over the expanse of the ocean. I thought about my new life sober and how it would last forever. Linda and Laura came into my mind; I knew I preferred Linda, but the sex was better with Laura. The confusion over women, and other things, felt new, even though it wasn't. I would have to tell Laura to stay away. I really wanted to settle down with Linda.

## Chapter Five

The guys were up when I returned. Eliot was making coffee, and George was in the shower.

"Did you hear anything last night?" I asked Eliot.

"Yeah, I heard everything; these walls are as thin as paper. You'd better be careful, Paul, you're treading on thin ice."

"I know. I'm going to tell Laura to stay away; I can't handle the chaos. I want some serenity in my life."

"You should have sent her away last night. What were you thinking?"

"I couldn't resist her; she's so sexy."

"She's going to make you relapse; you'd better watch out."

"You're right. I've already decided I'm in love with Linda, and that's it."

At least that was how I felt at that moment. I always seemed to sabotage myself when it came to women. Here was Linda, a woman any man would have been happy with, and I wasn't satisfied.

"What are we doing today?" I asked.

"You've got therapy this morning, and we're going to the beach as usual."

"Hey, is there a cappuccino for me?" George said. "You were having a good time last night. That Laura is a screamer; you'd better be careful."

"I already told him," Eliot said.

I called Linda to see if she was awake yet, and she was just getting out of bed.

"Hi, sleepyhead," I said.

"Good morning. What time is it?"

"Almost eight."

"How did you sleep?" she said.

"I slept well. How about you?"

"I tossed and turned all night," she said. "I dreamt that you had sex with another woman."

"It was only a dream, sweetie."

"I know, but I think my subconscious is telling me not to trust you."

"Is that why you tossed and turned all night?"

"I'm just kidding."

Suddenly, I had a fear that somehow she would find out about Laura. I knew the guys wouldn't say anything, but I didn't trust Laura. I resolved again not to cheat on Linda and told myself that it was really the last time.

"What are we doing this morning?" she asked.

"We have therapy. Then we are going to the beach; it's going to be a little cool, but it should be nice."

"What are you going to talk about in therapy?" she asked.

"I hadn't thought about it," I replied.

"Maybe I'll talk about my difficult childhood," she said.

"You never told me about that."

"I was molested as a child by my uncle and had forgotten about it for several years, until I went into therapy.

"I didn't even know you had been in therapy."

"For a little while," she said.

"Did your parents find out about your uncle?"

"Yeah, and they disowned him, but the damage had already been done."

"Do you think that's why you're a little reserved in bed?"

"I didn't know I was reserved. You never said anything about that."

I didn't want to hurt her feelings, so I didn't say anything more. Then I thought I would cover it up a little.

"You're only a bit reserved, which is normal for your age, but I love having sex with you."

"How am I reserved?"

"Well, you don't like anal sex," I said.

"That doesn't make me reserved; it makes me normal. You're perverted; that's all."

Now she was mad, and I didn't want to make it worse.

"Why don't you come over, and we'll have breakfast. The guys will be here for another hour or so."

"All right," she said, still pissed off.

I hung up and gave Eliot one of those looks that meant I had fucked up. He laughed and laughed. George had heard the conversation too.

"You told her she's reserved because she doesn't like anal sex?" Eliot said.

"Well, that's not the only way. I used that as an example."

"That was a stupid thing to say!" He laughed and said, "Now she thinks you're a pervert."

"It's not perverted, anyway; some people enjoy it."

"Whatever."

I made a cappuccino and ate a bagel, even though Linda was coming over for breakfast. Now I would have to apologize to her. I felt stupid, but I still thought she was reserved in bed. It didn't matter that much. Sex wasn't the reason that I loved her. She was leaving the next day, so I wanted to make this day perfect. I washed the dishes from the night before and cleaned up the rest of the kitchen.

"Why don't you guys hang around for a while? Linda's coming for breakfast."

"Don't you want to be alone with her?" George said.

"Actually, I'd rather have you guys around; it makes it easier to deal with her."

"Why do you have so much fear?" Eliot said.

"I don't know, but she's already angry with me; I don't want to make it worse."

I was not used to having so much fear, but I knew it was typical in early recovery. Linda was having trouble understanding the new me; she was used to a confident, self-assured young man. Half an hour later, she showed up, and she was looking as beautiful as ever. She had a sun dress on, which set off her tan nicely. She wasn't angry any more. I was relieved.

"Would you like a cappuccino?" I asked her.

"Desperately," she said.

"I'm sorry about what I said; I really am."

"I've already forgotten about it."

"Eliot laughed at me," I confessed.

"I don't blame him," she said.

I made the coffee and relaxed as Eliot and George picked up the conversation.

"So, you're leaving tomorrow," George said.

"Yeah, it's been great. I want to thank you for making my stay so interesting and enjoyable."

"Have you thought more about living out here?" Eliot asked.

"I've thought about it, but we haven't made any decisions. All I know is that I want to stay with Paul."

"Paul's going to stay. Aren't you, Paul?" George said.

"I don't know."

I sipped on my coffee and looked at Linda. At some moments, she was really breathtaking. I wanted to be with her, and at the same time, I wanted to be free, which I was accustomed to. I was not used to being tied down, though I liked having a girlfriend. Linda, on the other hand, wanted to get married and follow me anywhere.

"The life out here is more exciting. This is a perfect place for Paul to write and paint. We're close to L.A., and there are so many places to visit. You can even go skiing in the mountains," George said.

"It would be romantic," Linda said, glancing at me.

"Well, I'm going to be here for a few more months anyway. It'll give us time to think," I said.

I made some eggs and toast for Linda. She was a light eater in the morning. I just drank my latte; I often skipped breakfast. A couple of hours later, Linda and I went to therapy. We were early, so we talked to some of the other patients and their families. When the session began, I was feeling pretty good. We did our feelings check, and Linda said she felt nervous. I said I felt calm and collected, which was not a feeling according to the therapist, so I had to try again.

"I feel relaxed and confident," I said.

After going around the room and finding most people feeling pretty good, we got into the nitty gritty. Linda wanted to talk, so she went first.

"Paul said I was reserved in bed, which didn't make me feel good at all. I don't know what he wants from me; he has definitely changed since coming out here."

"How has he changed?" the therapist asked.

"He's more nervous and afraid. I've never seen him like this."

"Paul, how do you feel about what Linda is saying?"

"Well, I do feel more fear. In our meetings we discuss fear, and it's normal to feel that way at this stage of my recovery. I don't fear Linda. I just have some sort of undetermined fear. Sometimes, I wish I were dealing with this alone. They say you shouldn't have a relationship the first year or two of recovery. I need to work on myself."

Linda stared at me in disbelief.

"Do you really want to be alone?" she said.

"I do and I don't. I love you, but it's so hard to keep a relationship going when I feel so strange."

"How do you feel strange?" Linda asked.

"I don't feel comfortable in my own skin."

"What does that mean?"

"I'm so sensitive to everything."

"See, that's what I don't understand. He was never this way before."

I was at a loss. The people in my support group understood perfectly well what I was talking about, but Linda, a "normal" person, didn't understand any of it. The therapist, who was an alcoholic herself, understood perfectly, and tried to explain it to Linda.

"Paul's body is going through some major changes, chemical changes, and he's not his normal self. You're going to have to wait a few months until he adjusts," she said.

"I guess I can understand that, but now he's saying he wants to go through it alone."

Linda looked at me with despair; she was really at a loss, and so was I.

"I need some time is all. I don't want to separate from you," I said. "I want to stay in California for a few months and get my act together. Then I'll come back to Syracuse and we can start fresh. I still love you."

She seemed frustrated and didn't respond. She knew I had made up my mind and put her face in her hands. I wondered if she was crying, but I didn't hear anything. I felt bad, of course, but what more could I say? I wanted to go back to the halfway house and bury my head in my pillow. Linda lifted her face and shook her head.

"I guess it's best if we separate for a while; I don't think I can handle him anyways," she said.

"Well, I guess we've come to an agreement," the therapist said. "If you're meant to be together, you will be," she said.

Then I thought about losing Linda, and fear struck me again. What if we never did get back together? I would be giving up the best thing that had happened to me. Somehow, I wished I were already five years into recovery, and that Linda and I were married. We left the session and went back to the house. Conversation was very difficult, and we were lost in thought. I figured I had messed up everything beyond repair.

## Chapter Six

That afternoon, we went to the beach and hung out with the guys. Linda was unusually quiet, but Eliot tried to get her out of it.

"You guys must have had a difficult session. What's up?" he said.

"It looks like we're going to separate for a while," Linda said.

"Maybe it's for the best," he said.

"I guess so, but I'm not too happy about it," she said.

I rubbed some oil on her back and smiled at her. She wasn't to be consoled.

"I know it's frustrating," Eliot said. "We run into these problems all the time; it's common in early recovery."

"What is this early recovery bullshit?" Linda said. "You'd think it was the end of the world."

"It is the end of something," George said, "and it's the beginning of a new life. We don't expect you to understand."

"I really don't understand," she said.

I had never seen her so angry, and it hurt me to watch her like that. Now I knew she loved me; she fought the more she lost control. I didn't know what to say. I figured I had better keep quiet before she got angrier.

"You've got to give him time, Linda," Eliot said.

"In a few months, there'll be nothing left of our relationship," she said.

"Sure, there will. Paul can't live without you," George said.

Now Linda began to cry, not loudly, but silently, and it was really painful to watch.

"I can't take this," she said.

"Don't cry," I said. "Things will be better in a couple of months."

"I don't' think so," she said.

I rubbed her back some more and tried to console her.

"I love you, Linda. I'm not going anywhere."

"You'll be here in California, and I'll be back in Syracuse."

"I'll send for you as soon as I get out of the halfway house."

She stopped crying and gave me a kiss.

"Do you really still love me?" she said.

"Of course, I do; I want to marry you and have eight children."

She burst out laughing.

"I'm not having eight children; you're on your own."

The three of us laughed too, and the crisis was over. I wiped the tears off her face and gave her a big, passionate kiss. She smiled and kissed me back.

"You can be so difficult sometimes," she said.

"I know, and I'm sorry, but you wait a few months, and you'll see the new me."

"That's just what I'm worried about; I want the old you."

"I can't go back to that way of life."

"I guess you're right, but this transition period is impossible."

We lay on the beach under the hot sun and meditated about our lives. We had been thrown together by circumstance, and we felt lucky. I was excited about my new way of life, but was anxious for Linda to leave. I wanted to fight this battle with Eliot and George until I felt better. After a while, Linda went back to the hotel, and the guys and I went back to the house. What I had hoped would be a great day turned into a very difficult one. We made dinner and sat pretty quietly, eating. They knew I was in pain, and they didn't say anything. Laura came over later in the evening, but I sent her away.

I had a lot of trouble sleeping that night. The voices of the day echoed in my mind, and I tossed and turned all night. I got up early and took a very hot shower. George got up early too, and we made cappuccino.

"So, she's leaving today," he said.

"Yeah, I'm glad, too."

"I know how you feel; I'm having trouble with my wife as well."

"I guess I should be glad I'm not married."

"You really should be. I wouldn't mind being in your position. You don't have to work; you can concentrate on recovery, and you have a beautiful girlfriend."

"I do feel grateful, but I wish Linda understood better."

"Be glad she's normal. My wife is an alcoholic, and we haven't even begun to address her problems. She understands my problems and expects me to change, but isn't willing to change herself."

"I'm glad Linda's not an alcoholic. I hope she becomes more accepting of me. Now that I think of it, there are support groups for her, too."

"That's right, and if she really loves you, she'll stick by you."

We talked for another hour or so. Then I called Linda and told her I would pick her up to take her to the airport. As we drove along the coast, she was again taken by the great beauty.

"I really wouldn't mind living here," she said.

"Perhaps we will," I said.

"Oh, Paul, I hope we stay together. I really mean that."

"I hope so too."

We were silent for a long time during the drive; I dropped her off at the airport about an hour before she was supposed to fly.

"I love you," I said when I kissed her goodbye.

"I love you too. Call me tomorrow," she said.

I felt free on the way back to Oxnard. It had been a difficult week, but now I could relax. The drive back was exhilarating, especially since I had two double espressos on the way. I thought during that drive that I would definitely live in California for the rest of my life. When I got back, the guys were packing up to go to the beach.

"We brought your stuff too. We figured you'd go with us," George said.

"I'm in," I said.

"Now that you're a free man, what are you going to do?" Eliot said.

"I'm going to fuck Laura the first chance I get," I said, laughing.

"Not a bad plan," George said, "but you'll never get married," he added.

"One day I'll get married, but not yet."

I thought about Linda back in Syracuse and wondered seriously if I could ever marry her. Maybe I wasn't the marrying type. I knew that I was feeling free and didn't want to give up that feeling. We went to the beach, but it was cool out, so there weren't too many people. I felt secure being with the guys. They knew what I was experiencing and were there for me.

"Did Linda cry when she said goodbye?" Eliot asked.

"Well, there weren't any tears, but her face was pretty sad."

"She really loves you," he said. "You'd better not take that for granted."

"No, I won't; you're right, but I don't know if I can live up to her expectations."

"All you have to do is be there for her. You don't have to be a Superman."

I appreciated his soft tone and supportive words. He was a great friend, and I wasn't about to take him for granted. I looked out over the ocean. The surf was calm and the sun was directly above us. I wished I could feel that good every day.

"What do you think I should do about Laura?" I asked him.

"Whatever you want; you're a free man, but don't mistake rehab love for real love."

"What's real love? I like Laura. She's a great girl."

"Yeah, I like her too," he said.

"I'm going to see what she's up to," I said.

"You don't waste any time, do you?"

I walked back to the house and took a shower. The hot water felt good on my sweaty body. I put on some clean clothes and walked next door to see what the girls were doing. Laura was writing a letter to her father.

"Hey, what's up?" I said.

"Nothing, just sitting around; I'm almost finished with this letter. Hang on a minute."

I got a Pepsi out of the refrigerator and sat on the couch with her roommate in front of the TV.

"So, she left, huh?" Laura said.

"Yeah, just a little while ago."

"Now you're here bugging me," she said with a laugh.

"I can't resist you."

A few minutes later, she finished the letter, and we went for a walk.

"I can't play second fiddle to anybody," she said.

"I'm not asking you to. Linda and I are practically broken up."

"Practically? What does that mean?"

"I think I'm going to stay here in California, and she's going to stay in Syracuse."

"Did you actually come to that agreement, or are your bullshitting me?"

"No. We talked about it. She wants to stay there in school, and I want to start my life over again out here."

"We'll see."

We walked to the beach and sat on some rocks. I could see George and Eliot in the distance. I thought about Linda and how furious she would be if she could hear this conversation. I knew at that moment that Linda and I were finished. I was still too young to settle down, and I loved the chase.

"I know this may not seem important, but sex with you is much more intense than it is with Linda."

"That might be important, but what about our conversations?"

"I love talking to you. You're always funny, and I feel happy when I'm with you."

"I think you're fun too, and I especially enjoy the sex," she said.

"I know a relationship can't be based on sex," I said, "but the first part has to be intense, or it never takes off the ground."

"Sure, but it was intense for you and Linda too."

"It doesn't always last, of course, but I feel closer to you because you've been through the same ordeal that I have," I said.

"Maybe," she said, "but I did cocaine, you only smoked pot."

"It took us to the same place, and going through recovery together could be a wonderful thing."

I felt like I was trying to sell her a used car, and it wasn't working very well. I stopped talking for a minute and looked out over the ocean. Suddenly, above us I saw what appeared to be a hawk, circling and flying high above the gulls. I had always liked birds, so I followed this one on his lonesome journey. I was free, like this hawk, and flying higher than I had ever flown before.

"Listen, Laura, I'm not trying to pressure you into a relationship. I only wanted to let you know that Linda and I are through."

"I understand that, but why should I believe you?"

"Why would I lie to you?"

"To get into my pants!"

"I'm already getting into your pants."

"That's true, but I still don't believe you."

I watched the hawk dive down to the beach and pick up something in its beak.

"I told you about Linda from the beginning. Why would I start to lie to you now?"

"I don't know. I'm feeling very insecure today. I don't trust anybody."

"Well, you can trust me."

"Yeah, I've heard that before."

I wanted to end the conversation and go back to the house. I was feeling uncomfortable. The hawk had disappeared; it had probably flown up into the hills.

"I'm getting kind of tired, sweetheart. Can we walk back to

the houses?" I said.

"Sure."

I took a long nap and a hot bath, while Eliot and George were still at the beach. I felt comfortable being alone, but I knew that alcoholism is a disease of isolation. Having been with Linda all week had tired me out. After my bath, I got something to eat; I was beginning to get the hang of regular life, with regular meals and a decent amount of sleep. I sat in front of the television, not paying attention, and thinking about my life. The boys arrived later in the afternoon.

"What have you been up to?" Eliot asked.

"I needed to relax. I've been watching TV."

"Did you talk to Laura?" he said.

"Yeah, that's why I needed to relax."

"You always get yourself into trouble, but I like your style."

"I can't help it. I like fucking Laura too much."

"Linda is just as hot."

"I know, but Linda has less experience."

"That's not everything. You can give her the experience. She's not as wild as Laura."

"I like that wild streak in Laura," I said.

I put on a pot of coffee and heard the shower running. George liked to stay clean. I loved living with the guys; it reminded me of my fraternity days.

"A wild streak like hers could cause trouble," Eliot said. "You don't know if she can stay clean and sober."

"That's true. I never thought of it that way.'"

"I think you're better off with Linda, but I know it's none of my business."

"Of course, I appreciate your advice, but I don't know if I'm in love with Linda any more."

I poured some coffee for Eliot and me and heard the shower go off.

"Boy, that George loves to take showers," I said.

"I think you could be in love with Linda again," Eliot said, "but you have to go through recovery for a while until you settle down."

"Yeah, I'm still a mess."

George came out in his boxers with a towel around his neck.

"What are we doing for dinner?" he said.

"Let's go to the cafeteria. It's cheap, and we can see the new girls," Eliot said.

"Yeah, I can watch Laura eat lettuce for dinner," I said.

"What kind of eating disorder does she have?" George said.

"She's bulimic," I said.

"On top of an addiction? You'd better stay away from her," George said.

"But she's got such a great personality, and she loves me," I said.

"Linda loves you too," he said.

We got dressed to go to dinner. I wore my shorts and a nice shirt. I was beginning to dress like the Californians, very casually, and with bright colors. We were early when we arrived, so we sat at a table and talked.

"I like that new girl Janet," Eliot said.

"Invite her over to eat dinner with us," George said.

"What's wrong with her?" I asked.

"What isn't wrong with these women?" George said.

"I think she's into pills," Eliot said.

"What kind of pills?" I asked.

"I don't know, but she's awfully beautiful, don't you think?" Eliot said.

"Yeah, she's hot," George said.

Slowly but surely, people began to arrive for dinner. Some patients were in better shape than others, but after a couple of weeks, most of them started looking better. The food was served at five-thirty sharp, so we got in line early and waited. I was really hungry. We were having a choice of chicken or meatloaf, and I loved our cook's chicken, so that's what I picked. Eliot asked Janet to eat with us, and she accepted. There were five of us, including Laura.

"How do you like the rehab, Janet?" Eliot said.

"I'm just so glad to be clean. It wouldn't matter to me where I was, but it's beautiful here," she said.

"You'll get sick of it soon," Laura said. "The novelty wears off."

"How long have you guys been here?" Janet asked.

"A couple of months," George said.

"I see you have a ring on your right hand. Are you divorced?" Eliot said.

"Separated."

"Close enough," I said.

"You're strikingly beautiful," Laura said.

"Thank you. You're not so bad yourself."

"Do you two want to get together? Don't let us get in your way," Eliot said.

"I don't have a gay bone in my body," Laura said.

"Me neither," Janet said.

"This chicken is delicious," George said. "Let's take some back to the house."

"How are the halfway houses?" Janet asked.

"They're all right; the nice thing is we get to go to the beach all day," Laura said.

"I think I'm going to stay for six months," Janet said.

"I hope you do," Eliot said.

"You can hang out with us and go to the beach."

"This experience won't be as bad as I thought," Janet said.

"There's a lot of backstabbing gossip, just so you know," Laura said.

"I bet they're talking already," I said.

We ate our food, feeling like we were a group of old friends, and the time went by quickly. Laura put some chicken in her purse to take back to the house. Laura was very graceful. She had fine hands with long fingers and was very coordinated. She walked like a princess and measured her words carefully. I loved her ways.

"Am I allowed to look at your houses?" Janet asked.

"Sure, just tell one of the aides that you're not going to leave the property, and we'll show you around," Eliot said.

We all walked back to the houses in the warm sunshine. I couldn't help but think of Linda stuck in the wet spring weather of Syracuse.

"Come with me," Laura said to Janet.

"I hope they become good friends," Eliot said.

"You're only saying that so they'll hang out with us, and you'll get a shot at Janet," George said.

"Of course; I'm not a fool."

"Laura could use a good female friend," I said. "Sometimes, I think she feels left out when she's with us."

"Laura's a bit of a thinker, isn't she?" George said.

"Yeah, she's smart, but because of her addiction, she dropped out of school," I said.

"How much college does she have?" George said.

"A year and a half," I said.

"She's young yet; she can go back," Eliot said.

"I hope so, but she's got a kid, too. That's going to make it difficult," I said.

"You were smart to stay in school," George said. "That's one thing I don't like about myself; I don't have enough knowledge."

"You can go back to school; at least you can afford it," I said.

"I was never good in school," he said. "I don't think I can go back."

"I'm going back," Eliot said, "I'm studying counseling to get a job at a rehab."

"That's a good idea," I said.

"It's to meet women," George said, laughing.

"I admit it," Eliot said.

After a while, the girls showed up. The women were allowed in men's houses until nine o'clock, but they weren't allowed in the bedrooms, which didn't make any sense, but that's the way it was.

"I really like these houses," Janet said. "I hope I get a room to myself."

"Maybe you can stay with me," Laura said.

"That would be great," Janet said.

"Maybe you could stay with me," Eliot said.

"That would be even better," she said with a laugh.

I made some coffee. We were all addicted to it, and most of us smoked, too. I was really enjoying myself and thought that it would nice if Linda could be there as well. Laura was more of a party girl than Linda, and I knew that Linda would be better for me in my new life, but I was still attracted to Laura.

"You would corrupt her," Laura said.

"Listen, honey," Janet said, "I've already been corrupted."

"That's interesting," Eliot said. "We've both been

corrupted."

"You can always go lower," George said.

Janet had moments of shyness. She was still trying to get to know us. Eliot was deeply infatuated with her and paid a lot of attention to her. He was about fifteen years older, but neither of them seemed to care. Janet liked him apparently, because she responded to all of his advances.

"Where are you from?" Eliot asked her.

"San Francisco."

"Nice town," I said.

"There's so much to do there," she said. "Where are you guys from?"

"I'm from Ventura, right next door," George said.

"I'm from Syracuse, New York," I said.

"I'm from a small town near L.A.," Eliot said.

"I'm from Texas," Laura said.

"What an interesting combination!" Janet said.

I was listening to everything that was going on, but I was really thinking about having sex with Laura. She was wearing a short skirt and had long, slender legs.

"You seem so normal, Janet. Are you sure you're not just here to do a study on us?" Laura said.

"You guys seem normal too," Janet responded.

"I'm all fucked up," Laura said.

"You are not," I said emphatically.

"Let's go to the beach and watch the sunset," George said.

"Good idea," I said.

"But Janet can't come with us," Laura said.

"She has to go back anyway," Eliot said.

Janet went back to the rehab, and we walked to the beach. There were only a handful of people there, and the sun was a hot red. Eliot was smitten with Janet; he liked the way she wore her hair and the way she walked, as well as her personality. I held Laura's hand and talked to her while the guys walked along the shore.

"I want to kiss you," I said to Laura.

"You may," she said with a giggle.

I kissed her and thought I was in love. Now I was in love with two women at the same time again, and I was confused.

"I think we should have children," I said. "How do you feel about that?"

"Children, well, you don't waste any time, do you?"

"I love you."

"I love you too, but we're not even married yet; we haven't worked out the logistics of where we're going to live or anything. Why are you being so serious so soon?" she said.

"I don't know. I'm kind of manic, and I'm excited to be with you, so I'm being serious. Is that all right?"

"That's fine, honey. Settle down."

"I get emotional sometimes," I said.

It wasn't going as I had planned. I gave up a perfectly good relationship with Linda for an uncertain one with Laura.

"I think we should get married," I said.

"We need to spend more time together. You don't even know if you really love me."

"I do love you; I'm certain."

"You say that now."

We walked along the beach slowly, looking out over the placid water. The sun was beginning to set. The deep orange reflected off the water.

"I can't resist you," I said.

"There are a lot of relationships in rehab that don't work out.

We haven't gone through anything yet," she said.

"I know. I should slow down."

"I wish you would. I love you too, Paul, but for this to work out we have to do some careful planning."

"You're right, of course."

We walked back to the house and noticed that the coast was clear. We figured the guys would be at the beach for another hour, so we had time to make love. We jumped into bed and began kissing passionately. She liked to talk dirty in bed, and so did I.

"Fuck me," she said, "after you lick me."

I went down on her and remembered a technique I had learned in a *Playboy* article. I inserted one finger in her cunt and rubbed the G spot, while I licked her clitoris. It was making her go wild. She was so wet, and screaming out in ecstasy.

"Be quiet, honey. Somebody will hear us!" I said.

She rolled over on her stomach and stuck her ass in the air. She had a delicious, plump ass, and I started kissing it all over, moving down to her pussy.

"You bad little boy," she said. "You like that, don't you? You love licking my cunt."

I was hard as a rock, but I wanted her to suck me before I fucked her.

"Give me that cock," she said. "Stick it right in my mouth. I want you to come all over my face."

"I love fucking you," I said.

"I love sucking that big cock of yours."

I was about to come in her mouth when I had a big idea. I thought it would be cool to make her pregnant. I pushed her down and thrust my hard cock right in her cunt. I came deep inside her and said, "I'm coming, oh honey, I'm coming."

"Don't come inside me," she said.

"It's too late," I said.

"Paul! You know better than that. What if I get pregnant?"

"It's all right, honey. You won't."

She pushed me off her and got up.

"I can't believe you; for a smart person, you can be awfully stupid!"

"I'm sorry. I didn't know you'd react this way. Wouldn't it be nice to have a baby?"

"A baby! You're out of your mind!"

She got dressed quickly and stormed out of the house. I didn't know what to do. I thought she might be slightly dismayed, but I didn't expect that reaction. Then it occurred to me that I might have just made the biggest mistake of my life. Suddenly, I was gripped with fear. I tried calling Laura on the phone, but she didn't answer, which was probably good, because I didn't know what to say to her. A little while later, the guys arrived.

"You look like you've been through hell! What happened?" Eliot said.

"I think I just tried to make Laura pregnant."

"You think? You don't know?" George said.

"Well, everything was going fine, you know. I mean we were getting it on, and at the last minute, I thought it would be okay to come inside her."

"Did you tell her?" Eliot said.

"I told her after the fact."

"Boy is she pissed at you!" Eliot said.

"That's an understatement," I said.

"What are you going to do?" George said.

"What can I do? Pray that she's not pregnant and apologize to her."

"If she's pregnant, you're in deep trouble, buddy boy," Eliot said.

I tried calling Laura again, but there was still no answer. I was scared to death now and wished I hadn't been so stupid. A lot of different scenarios were running through my mind. I thought maybe she would want to have an abortion or give the baby up for adoption. I thought, on the other hand, how nice it would be to get married and keep the baby.

"Maybe you'll get lucky," Eliot said. "Ask her what part of her cycle she's at."

"I think she had her period a week ago," I said.

"Is she religious?" George said.

"Yes, I mean I don't know. Everybody in recovery seems religious to me."

"You'll just have to wait and see," Eliot said. "I made my first wife pregnant. That's how we ended up getting married. She was pissed too; I did exactly the same thing."

"My first wife trapped me," George said. "I thought she was on the pill, but she wasn't, and when she got pregnant, she told me her church insisted that we get married."

"I want to marry Laura," I said.

"That's what you said about Linda too," Eliot said.

"This time it's different. I never had the urge to make a woman pregnant," I said.

I tried calling again, but there was no answer. Now I thought I really did want to get married and have the baby. I was so confused. I was glad I had the guys there to bounce my ideas off of. They had more experience than I did in this area, and I looked up to them.

"Chances are she's not pregnant," Eliot said. "Have you ever made anybody pregnant before?"

"No."

"You don't even know if your machinery works," George said, "but it sounds like you want to make her pregnant."

"I do and I don't. I don't need to complicate my life right now, but I always wanted to have a kid."

"You're not in a position to have a kid," Eliot said, "but then neither was I. You'd better do some hard thinking about this."

A couple of hours later, I went to bed, but naturally, I couldn't sleep. I tossed and turned most of the night, but got a few hours of sleep early in the morning. I woke up exhausted.

## Chapter Seven

I decided to lie in bed, because I was too tired to get up. I didn't have anything to do, and I heard the other guys getting up and making coffee. I felt frustrated and angry with myself. I could hear George getting out of the shower, so I decided to get up and take one myself.

Eliot offered me a cup of coffee before I got in the shower, and I went outside to have a cigarette.

"Did you get any sleep?" Eliot asked me.

"Not much; I tortured myself all night."

"You can sleep on the beach later; it's going to be a hot one today," he said.

"A couple of cups of coffee will make me feel better," I said.

George came outside and lit a cigar. He looked like a big shot when he smoked.

"What a beautiful day!" he said.

"Yeah, for you," I said.

"You don't want to start your morning that way," George said to me. "You have to be grateful for what you have, and you've got a lot."

"I'll feel better after I take a nap," I said.

After my cigarette, I took a shower and shaved. I loved feeling the hot water on my body, but shaving every day was a nuisance. We got ready to go to the beach, but we planned on making a stop at Starbucks to see what girls might be there. Right before we left, the phone rang. George answered.

"It's for you," he said to me. "I thought it was Laura, but it was Linda."

"Hi, honey. How are you?" I said.

"I'm a mess, but that's all right."

"I'm sorry your visit had to be so difficult. It wasn't easy for me either."

"It's not your fault, but I'm exhausted and confused."

We'll work it out," I said. "I need a lot of time to adjust and to get my bearings. I still love you, of course, and I want to be with you if I can."

"I don't know if we can be together, Paul. I just can't get used to the new you."

"You keep saying that, but I don't know what you mean. I still treat you well, and I love being around you. What's the problem?"

"You seem to have a lot of fear that keeps your personality under wraps. I don't know how to describe it, but I definitely sense something different."

"That'll pass, sweetheart. You've got to give me a chance here. I'm still adjusting. I know you don't understand the process, but it's going to take time for me to get back to normal."

Suddenly, Laura came into my mind, and I got scared; what if Linda found out about my relationship with Laura? I started to stutter but pulled myself together.

"Listen, I've got to go. The guys are leaving for the beach. I'll call you later tonight."

George and Eliot laughed when I got off the phone.

"You're in deep shit, buddy," Eliot said.

"I know."

"This is typical early recovery," George said. "You are a mess."

"I can't help it, but at least it keeps life interesting. You guys wouldn't want me any other way."

They laughed, and we got ready to go to Starbucks. The sun was out as usual, but I was having trouble enjoying the nice weather, because my personal life was such a disaster. Eliot was more sympathetic than George. George thought I should marry Linda and be done with it. Eliot didn't care either way; he listened to me and tried to help.

"I'm getting a triple shot of espresso," I said.

"You won't be able to sleep on the beach if you do that," Eliot said.

When we got to Starbucks, I spotted Laura sitting with one of her girlfriends. She saw me and waved, but she had a very serious look on her face. Eliot turned around and winked at me. I wanted to talk to her but was afraid to. We got our drinks and went outside. It was a windy morning, but it was warm, and the girls were sitting only two tables away.

"She looks pissed," George said.

"I'm sure she is," I said.

"Don't worry about it. She'll get over it; my wife did the same thing," Eliot said.

"I hope she's pregnant," I said.

"You'd better not," George said.

"Why not? You both have kids, and I don't have any. It's about time I settled down. I think Laura and I make a good couple."

"Then why are you talking all that shit with Linda?" George said.

"If I can't make the decision myself, I'll let it be made for me," I said.

"That's stupid," George said. "Besides, you made the

decision to come inside her. Don't play innocent."

"Well, I really thought I wanted to make her pregnant. There's something to be said for the instinct to impregnate somebody."

"Well, you listen to yourself; you sound ignorant. That's something that has to be carefully planned out," George said.

"I guess you're right," I said.

I looked over at Laura, but she was ignoring me. She was smiling at her friend, but it didn't look sincere. I wanted to go over and talk to her, but I couldn't. I was so frustrated.

"Let's get out of here," I said.

"All right with me," Eliot said.

We got in the old Mercedes, and I took one last look at Laura. She was watching us drive away, and she didn't seem too happy.

The water was calm at the beach, and the sunshine glittered on the surface. I took my clothes off down to my boxers and ran into the water. It was so cold I could hardly breathe, and I rushed out immediately. I put my jeans on over my wet boxers while the guys were laughing at me. I loved being in California and thought I might stay there.

"Just because she might be pregnant doesn't mean she's going to marry you," George said.

"I know that," I said.

"You'd better hope she's not," Eliot said.

"What do you think she would do if she were pregnant?" I asked.

"Who knows?" George said.

"I doubt she would simply get married," Eliot said.

"She might," I said.

"Why do you want to get married so badly? You sound like a desperate man," George said. "Besides, I like Linda better;

she's more normal."

A few minutes later, we saw Laura and her friend Jenny walking up the beach. I was hoping they would come over, but they walked on by. I watched them go to the end of the beach where the rocks began, and then they turned around. The second time by, they walked up to us.

"What's up, guys?" Laura said.

"Relaxing," George said.

"Paul, can I talk to you for a minute?" she said.

"Sure."

We walked down the beach a little ways and talked.

"Listen, Paul, if I'm pregnant, I'm going to have an abortion."

"Don't do that."

"Be reasonable," she said. "We hardly know each other. Besides, my life is in Texas, and your life is in New York."

"Why can't we simply stay in California and make new lives for ourselves? How do you know you won't relapse if you go back?"

"I could relapse right here; that doesn't make any difference."

"But we can help each other out; two are stronger than one," I said.

"I'm not having your baby, but that doesn't mean we can't keep going out. I kind of love you, I do."

"Who would have thought that you would be the practical one? I guess even if you have an abortion, we can have a child later," I said.

"Of course."

"But how are you going to feel after you have the abortion? A lot of women get screwed up psychologically."

We had walked a long ways from our friends, but I was feeling better now that we were talking.

"I won't get screwed up any worse than I already am," she said, laughing.

"Well, we don't even know if you're pregnant yet; let's not put the cart before the horse."

"Let's go back," she said.

When we arrived at our little beach party, the others were munching on some chips and fruit. The sun was getting hot, and we were all practically naked. Laura and Jenny were wearing thongs and had taken their tops off. Jenny was a hot blonde with a firm, petite body. She was kind of quiet, but we could tell there was something brewing underneath. Eliot liked Jenny, but he played it cool by staying in the background. We didn't know much about her and were interested to find out more.

"Were you a drinker, Jenny? Or do you have some other kind of problem?" I asked.

"I took prescription pills; I'm a nurse, so I could get my hands on anything I wanted."

"How long are you planning to stay with us?" George said.

"Hopefully six months."

"Where do you live?" I asked.

"In Ventura, not too far from here. I hear you live in New York."

"Syracuse," I said.

As she was talking to me, she spread her legs, and I could see her pubic hair sticking out from her thong. She had nice smooth legs. I was guessing she was around thirty years old. She had nice, firm little tits with big nipples. I was wondering if she wanted to do a threesome with me and Laura, but I let that fantasy pass.

"Are you single?" Eliot said.

"Divorced."

"Kids?" George said.

"No."

"Tell us about yourself. We don't want to interrogate you," I said.

"Well, I'm thirty-two, and I was married for five years. My ex was a cocaine addict and spent all my money; besides that, he gambled. I'm what you call a co-dependent. I'm an enabler. I worked while he did his thing."

"And it lasted five years?" George said.

"Well, only the first year was decent. After that, it was a nightmare."

"Why did you stay with him after the first year?" I asked.

"Because I'm a good Catholic girl, and we don't get divorced. My parents wouldn't have approved of it, and for a while I thought it was wrong too."

"You're lucky you didn't have any children," Laura said, looking at me.

"I guess so, but sometimes I wish I had a child."

"There's still time," I said.

We went around the circle, telling our stories, and I think Jenny was relieved that our tales were just as bad as hers. Actually, I thought, her story wasn't too bad compared to ours. My story could have been a lot worse, but unlike Eliot and George, I never got caught possessing drugs.

"Do you have a boyfriend now?" Eliot said.

"No, my best friends were my pills. I tried going out with one guy, but he turned out to be just like my husband."

"Isn't that always the case!" George said.

"How long have you been divorced?" Eliot asked.

"About two years."

"How long have you been taking pills?" I asked.

"About five years."

"I used for about twenty years," Eliot said. "Don't feel bad."

"I smoked pot for about nine years," I said, "but I experimented with cocaine too, once in a while."

I felt very relieved that Laura and Jenny were talking to us, because I knew Laura was still angry. I didn't want her to have an abortion, but I knew it was probably for the best. I asked Laura if she wanted to get a hot dog, and she agreed.

"I'm glad you have a new friend," I said. "She seems great."

"Yeah, I really like her."

"So does Eliot."

"Oh really! Well, I guess I'll tell her that and see what she thinks."

"Don't tell her that; let him make his own approach."

"He hasn't said a word all day!"

"He's kind of shy around women he really likes."

"You're not?" she asked.

"What do you mean?"

"I saw you looking her over."

"That's only normal," I said. "You know I'm interested in just you."

"And Linda?"

"Linda's too conservative for me. I like your wild side."

"Yeah, but you can discuss all that intellectual shit with her."

"That's not what keeps two people together."

"Why not? You have the same interests."

"People are animals; they're attracted by animal instinct."

"Yes, but we think too. Reason plays a part in it," she said. "You and Linda have a lot to talk about; we're not simple animals."

"I know you can't separate reason from instinct, but I have a deep affection for your mind as well," I said.

"I know I'm smart, but I'm not book smart like you two."

"All I know is I want to be with you all the time," I said.

"And when you get tired of me?" she asked.

"I'll never get tired of you. That's why I wanted to have a baby."

"Forget the baby; you don't even know me. I'd drive you crazy. You're much more conservative than I am."

"You would loosen me up."

"I think you're better off with Linda; you're two of a kind."

"Why are you trying to talk me out of being in love with you?"

"You're not in love with me."

"Now you're trying to tell me how I feel."

I looked out over the ocean and watched the gulls flying together. Why was it so simple for animals to get back together, but not humans?

"I love you, Laura; I want to marry you."

"This is a fine time to propose, right in the middle of eating a hot dog!"

"We're on the beach. What better place to be?" I said disconcertedly.

"I love you, Paul, but I'm not ready to marry you, and I'm not ready to have your kid!"

# Chapter Eight

I felt devastated. We walked back to the group and lay down. I wanted to get high in the worst way but knew I had to survive these feelings. I was quiet while the others talked, and I noticed Eliot watching and suffering with me. I was getting very attached to Eliot. I had never met a more sensitive man. George and I were close too, but Eliot was older and more like a brother. I stared at Jenny's tits, just to make Laura jealous, but I knew it wasn't working.

"Did you ever cheat on your husband?" Eliot asked Jenny.

"A couple of times, when I was high," she said.

"Did he find out?" George said.

"Not really, but he suspected," she said. "He checked on me all the time."

"I've always cheated on my boyfriends," Laura said, looking at me.

"What about you, Paul?" George said with a laugh.

"We know his story," Laura said.

"I've cheated, but I've never gone out with somebody for a very long time and cheated."

I wanted to go back to the house. I was in turmoil, so I got up and started walking. The others were surprised and tried to stop me.

"Don't go; we're only kidding," Eliot said.

"I don't feel good," I said. "The heat is getting to me."

I walked home, feeling sorry for myself, and I knew at the

same time that I had no reason to feel that way. Fortunately, remembering my support group meetings, I knew the feeling would pass and that I would feel better in an hour or two. When I got home, I took a cold shower and went to bed for a nap. I couldn't sleep, of course, so I got up and wrote a poem. It was a piece of crap, so I threw it out and went to one of the houses next door to find one of my friends. He wasn't there; he was at a strip club apparently. I went back to the house and read, thinking about my friends. I felt better after a couple of hours and was happy to see George and Eliot return.

"We're sorry," Eliot said.

"No need to apologize; I was only feeling sorry for myself because Laura wouldn't get engaged."

"When did you ask her?" George said.

"While we were walking on the beach."

"What did she say?" Eliot said.

"She said no, in no uncertain terms."

"That's too bad," Eliot said.

"We're still going out though."

"You've got to take it easy, Paul," George said. "You're girl crazy. First Linda, then Laura; give your emotions a chance to settle down."

"You're right, of course, but I've never been so much in love in my life. I can't seem to relax."

I made some coffee and turned up the air conditioner. It was cool in the house, but I was sweating. I sat down and closed my eyes for a second.

"Maybe you should cool it for a while and not go out with anybody," Eliot said.

"You might be right," I said, "but I can't resist fucking Laura."

"She probably won't fuck you for a while anyway," George said.

"Why not?"

"She's angry," he said.

"Yeah, but she knows I love her."

"She doesn't trust you," Eliot said.

"You guys are making me angry," I said.

"Do what you want," George said. "We don't care."

"Why are you guys always telling me what to do?" I said.

"We're only trying to help," Eliot said.

"I'm going for a walk," I said.

I went outside and lit a cigarette, walking toward the beach. The sun was beginning to set, and it was a deep orange. It was beautiful out, and I felt better being on my own. I knew they were right, of course, but I still wanted to go out with Laura. I was thinking less and less about Linda, though I was still planning to return to Syracuse, at least temporarily.

I walked along the beach and calmed down. I began to feel a little joy, being in California, and being sober. After an hour or so, I returned to the house. The guys had gone to the cafeteria for dinner and had left me a note. It was getting cooler out, so I put on my jeans and went to have something to eat. The guys were sitting with Laura and Jenny, and they were laughing.

"There he is," Eliot said, as I approached with my tray in my hands.

"I'm sorry if I hurt your feelings," Laura said.

"That's all right," I said.

"Sit down. Jenny was just telling us about her kinky husband."

"How kinky was he?" I asked.

"He used to put my panties on," she said, laughing, "and

when he got a hard on, it popped right out of them!"

"That's not kinky," I said.

"Wait! It gets better," Eliot said with a laugh. "He used to stick her big toe up his ass!"

"Now that's kinky," I said.

"You've got to do a lot of cocaine to find that appealing," George said.

I felt better instantly.

"What else did he do?" I asked. "But you're kind of kinky too, Jenny; you were involved in all this."

"I was high too; I didn't care, as long as he gave me some attention. He always wanted me to lick his asshole."

"He had a little ass fetish," Eliot said with a laugh.

We talked more about sex, but I didn't let Laura share her experience with me, not that we were kinky in any way, because we weren't, but I didn't want her talking about it. George told us about a time when his wife tied him up and tickled him with a feather duster. Eliot shared about a time when he was with three women, but Jenny's stories topped the charts.

"I did a threesome too," Jenny said, "twice actually, once with another man, and once with another woman."

"Which did you like better?" Laura said.

"With the woman; two men is too much." She laughed.

"I can just imagine you," Eliot said, "but not with a toe up your ass!"

We all burst out laughing, and everybody in the cafeteria turned around. Jenny turned bright red, since Eliot had said it loud enough for everyone to hear.

"What was it like being with a woman; I've always wondered," Laura said.

"It was great while I was high, but the next day I was kind

of disgusted with myself," Jenny said.

"There's nothing wrong with it," Laura said.

"I know, but I'm not really interested in girls."

"I should have tried it while I was getting high; I don't think I could do it sober," Laura said.

"I hope not," I said.

"Oh, you would love it," Laura said.

"I don't think so," I said.

Laura gave me a look, and I shut up. Eliot couldn't stop laughing, and George had a big smile on his face. We were all glad that we had another woman in our group. Jenny fit right in. After dinner, we split up and went to our respective houses. I was tired and took a hot bath. The guys turned on the TV and vegged out. Most of my days were not as difficult as that one, but we ended on a good note, so I felt better. I went to bed early but tossed and turned for a long time, because I had drunk too much coffee. Finally, I fell asleep and had several horrible dreams. In the morning, I dragged myself out of bed and got in the shower. Eliot was already up.

"How did you sleep?" he asked.

"Terribly."

"Too much coffee?"

"Yeah."

"Me too."

After my shower, I went back to bed for twenty minutes and felt much better when I woke up. I don't know why, but I decided to call Linda. She was already back from her first class. I had forgotten about the time difference.

"Hi, sweetheart!" I said.

"Hey stranger, what's up?"

"Sorry I haven't called, but I've been busy with my meetings and stuff."

"That's all right. What's new?"

"I've decided to come back to Syracuse."

"That's great! Summer is almost here; we'll have a wonderful time."

I didn't really know what to say to her. Laura was running through my mind, and I felt weak emotionally.

"I miss you," I said.

"I miss you too. What made you decide to come back to Syracuse?"

"I feel lonely out here. I miss you and my mother and my brother. It's home for me."

"You're not going to change your mind again, are you?"

"No, at least not today," I said, laughing.

"I love you so much, Paul."

"I love you too. I've got to go now; I'll talk to you later."

"Okay. Goodbye."

I felt better just talking to her. I thought, *Fuck Laura*. Linda at least was as normal as a person could be, and she was doing something with her life. It was easier for me to talk to Linda; so what if the sex wasn't as good? That would wear off anyway.

I wanted to take another nap, but the guys wanted to go to the coffee shop, so I went with them. I had a triple shot of espresso in order to wake up, but even that didn't help.

"I talked to Linda this morning," I said, expecting the worst.

"I thought you were done with her," Eliot said critically.

"I'm going back to Syracuse."

"Here we go again," George said.

"You haven't made up your mind yet, have you?" Eliot said.

"I'm pretty sure."

"What did Linda say?" Eliot said.

"She still loves me."

"What about Laura?" George said.

"She's not for me; she's too crazy."

"Yesterday you asked her to marry you," George said. "You sound like the one who's crazy. I don't really mean that; I know you're confused. I've been there before."

"Don't be desperate, Paul," Eliot said.

"You've still got three months here. Make your decision at the end, after your emotions have settled down," George said.

"Thanks, guys. I appreciate your help. I don't know what I'm doing. One minute I want to marry Laura, the next I want to marry Linda."

"You're tired. Relax, don't think about it. Just worry about your sobriety right now," Eliot said.

I smoked another cigarette. I was smoking like a chimney and was operating on no sleep. We sat down outside, but there weren't any women from the halfway house. I simply wanted to go back to sleep.

"What did Linda have to say?" George asked.

"She was looking forward to my returning to Syracuse for the summer."

"It's summer here all year round," Eliot said.

"I know, but this isn't my home."

"You'll get used to it; it'll be your new home," George said.

"Besides, you've always said you needed a new start."

"I'm not in the mood to talk about it now; take me back to the house. I need to get some sleep."

They dropped me off at the house and headed for the beach. I took a hot bath and went right to bed. The coffee kept me awake for a while, but then I fell into a deep sleep. I dreamt crazy dreams about Laura and Linda and awakened with a start about six hours later. I didn't know where I was or what time it was; I was completely disoriented. Then it all came back to me, and I put my head on the pillow. I wasn't tired any longer, but I still felt like shit. I decided to get up and have some more coffee. After putting on a pot, I went out and had a cigarette. I was still thinking that I would return to Syracuse, if only to stay with my mother.

The guys came back about an hour later and said they had seen Laura and Jenny at the beach.

"Well, at least you look better than you did this morning," Eliot said, "clean shaven, hair brushed; you look good."

"I feel like shit."

"That happens a lot in early recovery; I was feeling like shit yesterday," George said.

"Did Laura say anything about me?" I asked.

"Yeah, she said she really likes you, but that you're too confused right now," Eliot said.

"No kidding. What else did she say?"

"She said she wanted to concentrate on sobriety right now, which is what you should be doing, and that she doesn't really need to be in a relationship right now."

"Fuck her," I said.

"Give her a break," Eliot said.

"I'm going back to Syracuse anyway," I said.

"She's probably going back to Texas," George said.

I made another pot of coffee and went outside to smoke a cigarette. I really didn't feel good. Never did I realize that my feelings would be in such turmoil. I was thinking of going over to talk to Laura, but thought better of it. *Maybe I should listen to somebody else for a change*, I thought.

Eliot decided to barbecue again, but I felt like going to the cafeteria. I walked to the rehab by myself and got in line. I saw

Laura and Jenny sitting on one side, so I went to the other. I sat with some guys that I knew but kept to myself. Laura came over a few minutes later.

"Why don't you come and sit with us?" she said.

"I don't feel good. I drank too much coffee."

"Come on. We'll make you feel better," she said, putting her hand on my shoulder.

I got up and went to sit with them. Jenny had a big smile on her face as I approached.

"Hi, Paul, how are you doing?" she said.

"Not too good," I said.

"I can understand that. Some days are better than others."

"Did you tell Eliot that you didn't need to be in a relationship right now?" I said to Laura.

"I didn't really mean it," she said.

"Then why did you say it? You knew it would get back to me."

"Don't take it the wrong way, Paul. You know I love you; it's just that they say one should stay out of a relationship for the first year."

"Then you do mean it."

"I don't know. Maybe we should give each other a little space; that's all."

"That's fine with me," I said as I got up and took my tray with me.

I didn't even finish my dinner; I walked out of the cafeteria and went back to the house. Eliot had made couple of extra pieces of chicken, and I ate one of those.

"The food wasn't any good tonight?" Eliot said.

"The camping wasn't any good," I said.

"Was Laura there?" he said.

"Yeah."

"What did she say?" George said.

"First, she comes over to my table and asks me to eat with her and Jenny. Then when I confronted her, she said she needed more space!"

"I told you," Eliot said.

"Big deal," George said.

"I'm going back to Syracuse," I said.

"As soon as the going gets tough, you want to run," Eliot said.

"I can't help it; Linda doesn't give me these problems."

"Does Laura know you're still talking to Linda?" George asked.

"I don't know. Did you say anything to her?" I said to Eliot.

"I didn't say anything."

"Then I guess she doesn't know," I said.

I devoured my piece of chicken, as if I hadn't eaten in three days. I was angry, depressed, anxious, and I wanted to leave California. I thought I would call Linda again but changed my mind.

"Why don't you give Laura some space like she wants? She'll come around; you've overwhelmed her," Eliot said.

"I'm going to have to; I have no choice."

"It's better that way," George said. "You need to settle down; you're twisted in knots."

"Yeah, I'm a mess."

After eating, I went back to bed. I tossed and turned for a long time since I had slept during the day, but eventually I fell asleep. I slept a long time and got up much later than usual.

## Chapter Nine

The guys had already gone to Starbucks when I got up. Eliot had left me a note. I had been a little over two months sober on that day, and I felt all the emotional upheavals of it. I decided to call my mother, as she always worried about me. We talked for about half an hour, and it was clear that she wanted me to return to Syracuse. I said I probably would, but that I hadn't decided for certain yet. I knew it was ridiculous to think that one woman would make me happy in one particular place, knowing my history. I merely wanted to be normal, whatever that was, and not have such severe mood swings. The guys returned, and they had brought me a latte.

My mother had sent me some money for a car, so we decided to go shopping that day. George knew a car lot that was reputable and had good deals on used cars.

"You should get something sporty," George said.

"I just want something reliable," I replied.

"I saw a nice old white Cadillac there," he said.

"How many miles on it?" I asked.

"A hundred and five, but those things will run forever," he said.

"I like Cadillacs," I said.

We got excited about the car and took off along the beach road. It was nice in the morning. There were only a few people walking along the beach with their dogs. The sun was creeping up the sky, and the few clouds passing by were puffy and light. I was feeling pretty good and tried to keep my mind off the women.

"How far is it?" I asked from the back seat.

"About twenty minutes," George said.

"How many cars on the lot?" I asked.

"Quite a few," he said.

I looked out over the ocean and thought it would be nice to live in California for the rest of my life. I thought about Syracuse and the long winters; I just wanted to escape. When we arrived, there were only two other shoppers, and the owner was the only salesman on the lot. I told him how much I wanted to spend and asked him what he had with less than sixty thousand miles on it. He showed me a few, but I didn't like any of them. Finally, I asked him about the Cadillac.

"Oh, you're going to like this one," he said.

It was a beauty, and the three of us piled in and took off. The engine sounded good, and the transmission seemed fine. When I brought it back, I let George haggle with him for a while. We got it down to three thousand dollars, and I bought it. I felt great. We had to leave it there until it got smogged and I got some insurance, so the guys and I drove back home.

"Now you won't have to rely on us to get around," Eliot said. "You can take Laura out for dinner or go to the beach whenever you want."

"I won't be taking Laura out for dinner anytime soon," I said.

"Yes, you will," Eliot said.

I was trying not to think about Laura, but now I couldn't help it. I hadn't made love to her for quite a while, and I was hornier than hell. I thought I would give her a few days to rest and think about us. She wanted space, so I would give it to her.

"I'm going to give her some time off," I said.

"Good idea," George said, "she'll come back to you if you

leave her alone for a while."

"What about Linda?" Eliot said, laughing.

"Linda and I are cool," I said.

"She wouldn't be too cool if she knew about Laura," Eliot said.

"She's not going to find out," I said.

"What does Laura think about Linda?" George said.

"I don't know. She thinks I'd probably be better off with Linda; we're more alike."

"I think so too," Eliot said.

When we got home, I took a short nap and felt good when I awakened. I took a shower and relaxed in front of the television. Nothing was on, of course, but this was my way of escaping. Frustrated, I turned off the TV and made myself a sandwich for lunch. I called about my car insurance and then called the dealership. The car was ready. Eliot and George were sleeping, but I wanted to pick up the car, so I woke up George.

"Can we go get the car now; it's ready," I said.

"Let me sleep for a few more minutes," he said.

Laura had a car, but I decided not to call her. I sat in front of a sorry-ass soap opera and waited for George to wake up. Finally, I woke him up again.

"Come on, George. I need to get the car."

"All right, all right," he said.

We got on the road, and I started to get excited.

"I can't wait to get this car. I'll be cruising."

When we arrived, I filled out the necessary paperwork, and the salesman handed me the keys. I was so excited that I gave George a big hug and hopped in the car.

"I'll see you back at the house, but it may be a few hours," I said.

I took off along A1A and looked at the sand that extended for miles. The car rode beautifully. I had to stop and fill up on gas. Fortunately, I had thought of bringing some money with me. I wanted to show Linda Santa Barbara and decided to cruise up there. It wasn't that far, and in a few minutes I was there. I parked the car along the street downtown and decided to eat lunch outside. There were two beautiful women sitting together at the table next to mine, and before long, we were chatting. One was named Sharon, with brown hair pulled back and delicate features; the other was named Heather, like my old girlfriend back in Syracuse, and she was a blonde with her hair cut short and bangs.

"Do you girls live around here?" I asked, thinking they were about in their late twenties.

"No, we're from Boston," Sharon said.

"I love Boston; I'm from Syracuse."

"Oh, I feel sorry for you," Sharon said with a laugh.

"But I'm thinking of moving out here."

"That would be a good idea," she said. "What kind of work do you do?"

"Well, I used to teach at Syracuse University, but now I've got some money, so all I do is write novels and paint."

"You've got it made," Heather said.

"Not exactly, but it's not bad. Writing is very difficult."

"How many novels have you written?" Heather asked.

"Five."

"Published?"

"Not yet."

"It's a tough racket," Sharon said.

"Lately, I've been doing more painting."

"Tell us about one of the novels you've written," Heather said.

"I'd be much more interested in talking about you," I said.

"We're dancers," Sharon said.

"Really? Ballet?"

"Modern."

"Wow, that's great!"

"We're starving artists," Sharon said, laughing.

"Well, you had enough money to make it out to the West coast."

"Barely, we drove here."

"That's adventurous."

"What are you doing out here?" Heather asked.

"I'm escaping for a while," I said.

"A girlfriend?" Heather said.

"Not really. I had a serious pot habit that I'm trying to overcome."

"I didn't know you could get addicted to pot," Sharon said.

"It's as addictive as any other substance," I said.

"We smoke some," Heather said with a giggle.

"Be careful," I said.

"We just smoke on the weekends, or when we take trips to California." Sharon laughed.

"Did you smoke some today?" I asked.

"Yeah, a little," Sharon said.

I felt very uncomfortable all of a sudden. Here were two beautiful women who had pot and wanted to show me a good time. I knew I was in trouble.

"Well, I have to go. You girls could get me kicked out of the halfway house I'm staying in."

"Oh, don't leave yet," Heather said.

"Why don't you come for a walk on the beach?" Sharon said.

"All right, I guess a little walk couldn't hurt," I said.

I was thinking that it was about four in the afternoon, and the beach was practically empty. We drove down there in my Cadillac. I wanted to show off my new car. They were giggling and carrying on like kids, and I was thinking that I would get laid by both of them. I parked, and we walked down to the water. Sharon took out a joint, and she passed it to Heather. Heather took a hit and passed it to me. Without even thinking, I took a drag off the joint and inhaled deeply. I got high off that one hit, probably because I hadn't smoked in a couple of months.

"No big deal," Heather said, looking at me. "They won't be able to trace that."

"I hope not," I said.

Suddenly, I was very disappointed in myself. I had failed a test. All the words that had passed in my support group meetings now flowed through my head. I was scared, and the high was not the same.

"Take another hit," Sharon said.

"No, thanks," I said.

"Come on, Paul; it's not going to hurt you," Heather said.

"No, thanks."

We walked along the beach, and all I could think about was showing up high at the halfway house. George and Eliot would be so disappointed. I decided to stay away until the drug wore off. I still wanted to fuck them, so I talked them into going back to their hotel. They finished the joint as we piled into the Cadillac.

"Did you get high, Paul?" Sharon said.

"Yeah, I did. It's been so long since I smoked that I got high off one hit."

"Good, then we can take advantage of you," Heather said.

"I'm up for that," I said.

We parked a little outside of town in front of a rundown motel.

"We couldn't afford anything better," Heather said.

"It's clean though," Sharon said.

Inside, I was surprised to find only one bed. Sharon sat down at a little desk and rolled another joint. Heather simply started taking her clothes off. Not needing any prompting, I took my clothes off. Sharon lit the joint and passed it to Heather. I was really tempted to take another hit but thought better of it. After Heather took a hit, she got down on her knees and started sucking my cock. It felt like the old days, and I just watched her pretty face take in and out my hard cock.

Sharon took her clothes off and put her arms around Heather, grabbing her breasts. Sharon had a shaved pussy, while Heather was nicely trimmed. Just before I came, I took Heather's mouth away and pushed her down. I started fucking her, while Sharon put her cunt on Heather's mouth. Sharon came quickly, and I kept fucking Heather until I came. I squirted my come in Sharon's mouth and fell back exhausted. The girls went at it for a while as I watched. I could feel the pot wearing off and thought about my trip back to Oxnard. After the girls were done, the three of us hopped in the shower and washed each other off.

# Chapter Ten

I said goodbye and got in my car. I wasn't really high but felt strange. I wasn't feeling like myself and wondered if the guys would notice. I decided I would go to bed immediately and sleep off the rest of the effects. I drove along the beach in my new Cadillac and became determined again to stay clean and sober. The car performed beautifully. I just cruised along, almost without a care. When I got back to the house, the guys weren't even there. I was relieved, of course, and went right to bed. I was exhausted from the sex and fell asleep almost immediately. When I awakened, I heard somebody in the kitchen.

"Hey, what's up, Eliot?" I said.

"Nothing. How's your car?"

"Great! I went up to Santa Barbara and cruised around. I sat outside and had something to eat."

"When did you get back?"

"About an hour ago, I guess."

"Did you talk to Laura?"

"No. Why?"

"She wanted to talk to you."

"What about?"

"How am I supposed to know?"

"Okay. Thanks."

I went next door and knocked. Laura came to the door in a bra and panties.

"Let me put something on. Come in," she said.

"You don't have to get dressed on my account," I said.

"I'll only be a minute."

She came out of her room a few minutes later, wearing a lovely white sun dress.

"Did you want to talk to me?" I said, still feeling some anger.

"I want us to go out again," she said matter-of-factly.

"Why the turnaround?" I asked.

"I've had enough time to think," she said.

"I thought I was crazy!" I said, laughing. "Anyway, I still need more time."

"Are you kidding? You were all over me," she said.

"Well, things have changed."

"Like what? Linda?"

"No. Not really."

"Then what?"

"I don't know if I want to be with somebody who suddenly breaks it off with me for no reason."

"I didn't break it off. I only said I needed a little space."

"Well, I'm giving it to you."

"You're impossible. Get out of here."

I left with a little smile on my face and felt a lot better. I told Eliot what had happened, and he said, "You blew it."

"I don't care; I'm thinking I don't really need to be in a relationship."

"That's the smartest thing you've said in a while."

I was tempted to tell him about the hit of pot I took, but was afraid of his reaction. We got tested every few days, and I was worried that we were going to be tested the next day. I didn't think it would show up on the test, but you never knew. Stranger things had happened.

"What do you hear from Linda? Are you going to break it

off with her too?" Eliot said.

"No, I'm sticking with her, but I haven't heard anything. I hope she's not mad at me."

"Why should she be mad at you?"

"Who knows why women get mad? They just do," I said.

"You don't sound like yourself," he said.

"I'm under a lot of stress."

"You usually handle it better."

"Yeah, I know; I'm going back to bed."

I took a hot bath and went to bed. I missed dinner, but didn't care. I had eaten enough at lunch. I thought about Sharon and Heather and wished I had never met them. After an hour of tossing and turning, I finally fell asleep. I had a strange dream that I was making love to Laura and Linda at the same time, and that Laura stabbed Linda at the end. I woke up after the dream, in the middle of the night, and decided to watch television. There was nothing on, so I went back to bed where I tossed and turned for the rest of the night.

In the morning, I felt like shit and went outside to smoke a cigarette. The air was clean, and here I was polluting my lungs with smoke.

I could hear George getting into the shower, and Eliot making some coffee. After the cigarette, I went into the kitchen to talk to Eliot.

"How did you sleep?" he asked.

"Not very well. I don't feel good."

"Why don't you go back to bed?"

"No, I'll have some coffee. That'll make me feel better."

"Are you going to drive your car to Starbucks or ride with us?"

"I think I'll drive."

"Why don't you call Linda later to let her know how you're doing?"

"You really think I'd be better off with Linda, don't you?"

"Yes, I do; you don't know if Laura can stay sober, and she might put your sobriety into jeopardy. She's very unpredictable."

"That's what I like about her."

"I know, but you're being foolish."

"Well, why don't you let me know how you really feel," I said, laughing.

I began drinking my second cup of coffee. I was thinking he wasn't being his usual supportive self. He was probably right though. Linda was the safe choice, and she had a lot of growing to do. I could help her grow, and we could develop together.

"Why can't I accept Linda the way she is, which is terrific, and be with her?" I asked.

"You have the grass is greener on the other side disease," he said.

"I wish I could combine the best features of each woman, but choosing between them seems impossible."

"Choose now before you lose them both."

"I can't even handle one, much less two," I said.

George had finished taking his shower and wanted to go to Starbucks. Just as we were leaving, the manager of the houses came over and told us we had to take a drug test. My heart leaped into my throat. We filed over to the rehab and took the test. I pretended to be as cool and calm as possible. We wouldn't get the results until the next day, so we left and went to our cars. Eliot decided to ride with me.

"George is having problems with his wife," Eliot said as we took off. We coasted along the beach and looked out over the ocean.

"What's the problem?"

"He wants her to go into rehab and quit drinking, but she doesn't want to."

"How much does she drink?"

"I think she drinks quite a bit, but she doesn't do drugs any more."

"It's still bad though," I said, wondering if Laura would be able to stay clean and sober.

"He can't control her, no matter what he thinks," Eliot said.

"No, she has to decide for herself," I said.

The sun was coming up above the mountains, and the light was a bright yellow. The blossoms were everywhere, and I was glad again to be in California. I somewhat worried about the drug test, but was fairly confident that nothing would show up. I was not ready to leave California. I needed a few more months.

"George knows all that; he's frustrated because he can't do anything about it," Eliot said.

"I thought I had problems. Plus, he has kids with her; it's not as if he can just leave. We have to be very supportive and try not to give him too much advice," I said.

"Besides, you're in no position to give advice," he said.

"No, I know that."

I frowned and thought that he was in no position to give advice either. We arrived at the coffee shop and discovered that Laura and Jen were there. I knew Eliot would want to talk to Jen; therefore, I couldn't be rude and not talk to Laura.

"What's up, girls?" Eliot said.

"Nothing," Jen said. "Did you guys have to take a piss test today?"

"Yeah, no big deal," he said.

"No, I'm not worried; it's just a pain in the ass," she said.

"It's so degrading."

"A guy got kicked out last week for testing positive for cocaine," I said.

"People get kicked out all the time," Laura said.

I noticed a tone of discord, but I wanted to be friendly with her. I still didn't feel comfortable about the test, and I knew it was a bad time to get kicked out. I was not stable.

"We have nothing to worry about," Eliot said. "All we have to do is stick together," he added, staring at me.

"I have no desire to use again," I said.

"I wish I were that confident," Jen said.

"We have to keep working on it," Eliot said, "a little bit of work every day."

I thought about Heather and Sharon and wished again that I had never met them. I felt like I had let down my friends and was resolved more than ever to keep my end of the bargain.

"Are you guys going to the beach?" I said to the girls.

"Sure," Jen said. "What about you?"

"I might go back to bed for a while," I said. "I didn't sleep well last night."

"George and I are going," Eliot said.

"I like your new car," Jen said to me.

"Thanks. I like it too."

"Well, we'll see you later," Laura said, as she got up.

"Can I talk to you for a second?" I said to her.

"We can talk at the beach later," she said.

I knew I had fucked up our relationship, but there was always hope that I could mend it. I still cared for her; actually, I felt that I still had stronger feelings for her than for Linda. George hadn't said a word the whole time. He was in his own world.

After the girls had left, I said to George, "Are you all right?"

"Not really," he said.

"Want to talk about it?"

"Not really."

"It's better if you talk about it," Eliot said.

"I can't understand why my wife won't go into rehab. I made a commitment to her, and I'm sticking to it. Why can't she do her part?"

"Maybe she's scared," I said.

"I was scared; it didn't stop me," he said.

"You don't know what she's going through," Eliot said. "Just because you're quitting, it doesn't mean she's going to."

"I know what she's going through. I went through it myself. You don't know what you're talking about," George said.

"I didn't mean to get you upset," Eliot said.

"I'm not upset at you guys; I'm frustrated is all."

"Things will work out; you'll see," I said.

"It's been going on for a long time," he said. "I'm losing hope."

We sat quietly for a while, and I was thinking that I had a lot of hope for the future, but I was still disappointed that I had smoked. The sun was getting hotter, and I was feeling more tired. I told Eliot that I was going to bed and to get a ride with George. I got in my car and cruised along the beach. I was so grateful that I wasn't married and in George's predicament.

I went to bed and fell asleep immediately, even though I had a lot of caffeine in me. I had strange dreams, but they were all disjointed, so I didn't remember anything when I woke up. In the afternoon, I took a shower and got in my car. I was thinking of meeting my friends at the beach but decided to drive along the coast instead. I kept driving and driving, thinking about Laura and Linda. Now I wanted to be back in Syracuse in the worst way and sleeping with Linda. I got back to the house about dinner time, and the guys were barbecuing.

"Where did you go?" Eliot asked.

"I drove north about a million miles and didn't do anything but meditate. I'm thinking that you're right about Linda; she's better for me. Laura's too crazy."

"Now you're thinking straight," Eliot said.

"What made you finally come to that conclusion?" George said.

"I feel more at peace with Linda, and I heard somebody say in a meeting that the most desirable thing in the world is peace of mind," I said.

"I wish I had some of that right now," George said. "I called my wife this afternoon, and she was drunk. My spirits fell through the floor."

"That's too bad," I said.

"She might come around eventually," Eliot said.

"I don't know," George said. "Now I'm thinking that I have to get divorced. I can't go on this way."

"Now that you're clean and sober, she might follow suit," Eliot said.

"She can't do it without rehab, and I don't even think she wants to quit," George said.

"She has to hit her bottom," Eliot said.

"But I'm enabling her; she can't hit her bottom unless I leave her," George said.

"That's probably true," I said.

We ate the ribs they had cooked, and they were delicious. I always ate quickly, and I got sauce all over my face. The guys laughed at me. Just then, the manager of the houses came by and told us we had all passed the drug test. I was so relieved, but I played it off as if it weren't a surprise.

"I think I'm ready to go back to Syracuse," I said.

"Every day it's a different story," Eliot said. "Why don't you stick around for a while and get used to living out here? I thought you were sick of Syracuse winters?"

"I am sick of the winter, but I miss my family and Linda."

"We've heard all this before. You like it better out here. Now that you've got your car, you can cruise along the beach. All you need to do is settle down a little," George said.

I ate about five big ribs with potatoes and spinach. All I could think about at that moment was being home. I wanted to be in my old apartment with my paintings hanging up all around me and with my new friends that I would make as soon as I got there.

"We're your new sober friends. You'd miss us if you went back to Syracuse," George said.

"I think I'm going to marry Linda, if she'll have me," I said.

"I thought you said you didn't need to be in a relationship right now," Eliot said.

"But I'm lonely," I said.

"How can you be lonely with us around all the time?" Eliot said.

"I don't know. I miss Linda."

We cleaned up the dinner dishes. George washed while I dried. We decided to go to the beach again in the evening, but I was thinking that we should take the girls with us. Eliot went next door and asked the women if they wanted to join us at the beach. They agreed.

# Chapter Eleven

We decided to all go in my car, and for the first time in a long time, I felt cool. Laura sat next to me, while the other three got in the back. Of course, the beach was only two blocks away, but we decided to go up the coast a ways to a nude beach. We drove for about half an hour and found the beach with no problem. The sun hadn't set yet, but there were a few campfires around with several people eating and drinking.

"What would your wife say?" Laura said to George as we walked to a deserted spot.

"She wouldn't care, as long as I look but don't touch," he said, laughing.

We took all our clothes off, and I noticed Eliot staring at Jen. She did have a beautiful body, but she wasn't as hot as Laura.

"I wish I could have a beer," Jen said, "just one."

"Yeah, sure, one or two," Eliot laughed. "You've got to stop thinking that way or you're going to relapse."

"I'm really only kidding," she said.

"Do you want to wade in the water?" I asked Laura.

"Sure."

Laura and I walked down to the water, gazing out over the expanse of the ocean and the glittering reflection of the falling sun. I was feeling very horny, so I wanted to get her under the water, even though it was pretty cold.

"You wanted to talk to me," she said.

"I would like us to get back together and not play any games.

I'm getting too old for that," I said.

"I still love you, Paul."

I pushed her into the water and jumped on top of her. As soon as I got wet, my cock shriveled right up. We started laughing hysterically as we played in the ocean. I was so happy then and wanted that feeling to last forever. I grabbed her by the legs and pulled them apart, sticking my foot right in her crotch.

"I love you," I said, as I let her go.

"Let's get married," she said.

"Do you mean it?"

"No. Yes, of course, I mean it. I don't take those things lightly."

"I'll have to think about it," I said with a laugh.

I pulled her toward me and went under the water to lick her pussy. My cock got hard as I shoved my face in her cunt.

"Do you really want to get married?" I said, after I came to the surface.

"I said yes."

"Where are we going to live?" I asked.

"Here in California. Where else? We can both get a new start."

"I would like to live in Santa Barbara," I said.

"Wouldn't that be wonderful?"

I looked up at our friends on the shore and yelled out, "We're getting married!"

Eliot and George waved and yelled out," Good for you."

I grabbed Laura and bent her over under the surface. I tried sticking my hard cock in her pussy, but she had to help me. I didn't care what anybody else thought, I wanted to fuck her right there. She rubbed my balls as I thrust it in and out. It wasn't long before I came, and I grabbed her hair as I climaxed.

"I really love you," I said, in the heat of the moment.

"You came quickly," she said.

"I was very excited."

"Do you think they could tell we were fucking?" she asked.

"Who cares?" I said.

We got out of the cold water, got our towels and walked up to our friends. Eliot, George, and Jen were laughing as we approached.

"Hey, what were you doing in there?" Eliot said.

"We were talking," I said, laughing.

"I'd like to talk to Jen like that," he said.

"Feel free," I said.

"That's no fair," George said. "I don't have my wife with me."

"Come on," Jen said, grabbing Eliot by the hand.

They walked down to the water, and the three of us laughed as Eliot's fat ass wiggled behind him. She dragged him out into the cold water and dove underneath the surface. He turned around, looking at me, and raised his hands in the sky. We laughed and laughed. After a while, they came back, and we teased them.

"Eliot can't get it up in that cold water," I said. "He was faking it."

"She can hold her breath a long time though," George said.

"I can do it longer," Laura said.

"Is that true, Paul?" Eliot said.

"She's magical," I said.

We built a fire by borrowing wood from our neighbors, and I was thinking that a joint would be perfect at about this time. I swiftly put that thought out of my mind. I was wondering if the others were having thoughts like that.

"It's getting colder out; I'm going to put on my clothes," Laura said.

"Me too," Jen said.

We watched the sun set over the glittering ocean, and I was at peace for one of the rare moments in my recovery. The three of us put on our clothes too, and we started telling stories around the campfire. About an hour later, we decided to go home. We cruised along the shoreline, looking at the few boats sitting calmly on the water.

# Chapter Twelve

It got quite a lot cooler as we arrived at the houses. I kissed Laura goodnight and told her to expect me in the middle of the night. The guys were very curious as we walked into the house.

"How did you ask her to marry you?" Eliot said.

"She just said it. I didn't even ask her this time."

"You're kidding?" George said.

"No. She blurted out, 'Let's get married!'"

"And a couple of days ago she wanted more space. You guys are crazy!" Eliot said.

I laughed but realized we were acting crazy. I knew these rehab relationships never worked out, but I was in the middle of one, and I wasn't going to let go. I was trying to put Linda out of my mind, but she kept creeping in. Linda was far more stable than either Laura or I, and was probably better for me, but I didn't listen to my own good sense.

"I know you prefer Linda, Eliot, and you're probably right, but Laura has a special something."

"Yeah, she's good in bed, but that wears off; take it from me."

"I know that wears off, but that's not it. She's more exciting in every way," I said. "Anyway, I'm going to marry Laura."

"Why don't you do yourself a favor and live with her first. You shouldn't marry her right away," George said.

"I've thought about that too," I said, "and you're right; I've got too much money to lose to get married right away."

I was so excited, I decided to make some coffee and stay up until I visited Laura. Eliot drank some coffee with me, while George went to bed.

"What are you going to tell Linda?" Eliot inquired. "Have you thought about that?"

"I'll tell her I'm in love with somebody else; she's young, she'll get over it."

"I've been cruel before myself," he said. "I guess I shouldn't say anything. I think you're going to regret this decision though; Laura is very flighty."

"She's young. She'll grow out of it. I'll help her grow."

I put the radio on quietly to the jazz station and was pleased to hear the comforting tones of a Miles Davis ballad.

"What about you and Jen?" I asked.

"We're getting along fine, but she has a lot of issues."

"So do you, don't you?"

"That's why I'm not sure I want to take on a relationship."

I glanced at the clock. The dorm manager would be asleep now. I was getting ready to go over and see Laura.

"You've got to take on a relationship sooner or later," I said.

"I guess you're right, but I don't think I'm ready yet. I do like her though."

"Why don't you ease into it and see how it works out?"

"I guess I could," he said.

"Well, I'm going over to see Laura. Do you want to come with me?"

"Sure. Why not?"

It was a cold night, and we were wearing sweatshirts with light jackets. We snuck over to the women's house, and I knocked gently on the door. A few seconds later, Laura opened it.

"What are you doing here, Eliot?"

"I came to see Jen."

"She's sleeping."

"Well, wake her up," I said.

"We're going to get caught with all this noise," she said.

"Let us in; we'll be quiet," Eliot said.

She opened the door and let us in. We couldn't turn on a light, so we stumbled through the house. Laura showed Eliot Jen's room, and then she took me into hers. We could hear Jen wake up startled, and we hoped nobody heard her. The manager's house wasn't that close. I wasn't too worried. Laura was nervous. I could tell. I started to take my clothes off, but Laura stopped me.

"I only want to talk," she said.

"All right," I said, disappointed.

"I want us to be married as soon as we get out of this place," she said.

"Do we get married in Austin or in Syracuse?"

"I think we should have a ceremony in both places, don't you?"

"I guess so, but we don't want to burden our families with an expensive wedding," I said.

I was rubbing her ass as we talked and had a wicked hard on. I thought maybe that after we talked, we could fuck.

"We'll just have the family there," she said.

"But shouldn't the two families meet?" I said.

"I guess you're right, but here?"

"I think Texas would be best."

I began pushing my cock against her, hoping to make her horny.

"Maybe you're right," she said. "I'm calling my mother in the morning, so you'd better not change your mind."

"I'm not going to change my mind."

I thought instantly of Linda, but put her out of my mind immediately. I wanted to live in California with a new sober life and lots of hope for the future. I grabbed Laura's breast, but she pushed my hand away.

"Oh, come on. Let's make love; we're engaged now!"

"I'm not in the mood; I have a lot of planning to do."

"You can't start planning in the middle of the night. Anyway, you should be planning on how to make me happy."

"It's easy to make you happy."

I could hear Eliot and Jen making love. Jen was pretty loud. I decided to go back to the house since I wasn't going to get any sex. I went to sleep almost immediately and dreamt strange dreams.

## Chapter Thirteen

In the morning, I woke up refreshed and got in the shower. Eliot was already up, and after my shower, I got a cup of coffee. I went outside to smoke my cigarette, thinking how much I was a creature of habit. The days were beginning to pick up momentum. I was not longer counting the hours. I set my sobriety date to the day I smoked the pot, thinking that at least I had to be honest with myself. As I was smoking my cigarette, I could hear George getting in the shower. Eliot always showered in the afternoon, which I thought was odd. I went inside and began talking to Eliot.

"Are you absolutely sure you want to marry Laura?" he said.

"As sure as I can be."

"What does that mean?"

"Well, I haven't known her for too long, but my feelings for her are intense."

"Doesn't it bother you that you've only known her for a couple of months?"

"People have married sooner than that and stayed married for fifty years."

Eliot had managed to put some doubt in my mind. I thought it might be better to live with Laura for a couple of years before getting married.

"There aren't too many couples today that are successful. It's not like the old days," he said.

"I think I'll live with her for a while."

"That's a better solution, especially the way you change your mind."

"I'd better tell her right way. She's calling her mother this morning to give her the news."

I walked over to Laura's house, and was glad to find her still sleeping.

"Wake up, sweetheart," I said.

"What are you doing here?" she said.

"I have to talk to you."

"What about?"

"Before you call your mother, I think we should talk about this marriage business."

"Don't tell me you've changed your mind already?"

"Not really, but I think we should live together for a while before we get married."

"But we're still engaged?"

"Yes, of course."

"Oh, that makes sense, but I'm still calling my mother."

"That's fine."

I left, thinking I was glad I got that off my chest. I was definitely afraid of commitment, and this time was no different. I had broken off an engagement years earlier, though I sometimes regretted it. I went back to the house and ate breakfast with the guys. I never ate much of a breakfast and often skipped it altogether. I saw a beautiful bird sitting on our windowsill and thought about my bird poems. I knew I had to call Linda sooner or later, but was afraid to. I didn't know what I'd say to her.

"What are we doing today?" I asked.

"The girls are meeting us at the beach," Eliot said.

"So, what's Jen like in bed?" George asked him.

"I'll never tell," Eliot said, laughing.

"Is she kinky at all?" George said.

"A little," Eliot said.

"Well, give us some details," I said.

"She likes it when I stick my finger up her ass while I'm fucking her," he said.

"Maybe she likes two guys at the same time," George said with a laugh.

"You won't be one of them," Eliot said.

"That's not kinky anyway," I said.

"No, I don't think so either," Eliot said.

"I noticed she makes a lot of noise," I said.

"Yeah, I thought we were going to get caught," he said.

"I have to call Linda," I said.

"Don't call her yet," Eliot said.

"You're probably right," I said.

"He's right," George said. "You'll break up with her, get her all upset, and then next week you'll have to try to get back with her."

"I'm pretty sure this time though," I said.

"Oh, please," George said.

"No, really," I said.

"Whatever," he said.

"Leave him alone," Eliot said. "You've been confused before; you took on a lover while you were married."

"I guess you're right," George said.

"Let's get going," I said.

We packed some things in George's van and went to the beach. The water was calm as usual, and the sun was creeping up. I felt happy, but was not looking forward to talking to Linda. I was thinking that perhaps I could ignore her and the problem would go away, but I knew she would call me soon. I walked along the water while the guys lay on the beach. I wanted to escape, to get high, and forget all my problems.

The girls showed up a few minutes later, and Laura wanted to tell me about her wedding plans, even though it had been postponed. We walked along the shore together, and I was glad she was with me.

"I talked to my mother this morning," she said.

"What did you tell her?"

"I told her I was engaged to the most handsome man in the world!"

"Thanks, sweetheart, but she must be really concerned since we're both in a halfway house."

"She knows I'm crazy, but she also knows that I rarely get serious."

"You're not crazy; quit talking like that."

"We're both crazy in a way, but in a good way."

"I'm not crazy, even though I've had problems," I said.

"You had a nervous breakdown," she said. "That's not crazy?"

"Yeah, but I recovered one hundred percent. I'm not crazy now, just confused."

"Confused, crazy? What's the difference? Don't be so sensitive; everybody is crazy!"

The warm sand felt good under my feet. The sun was heating up the air as well. I looked out over the ocean and noticed boats lazily floating. At that moment, I was glad to be right where I was, a rare moment.

"So, what else did you tell her?" I asked.

"I told her you have a master's degree in English Literature, that you're a writer and a painter, that you have a great sense of humor, and that you're sweet, the most important ingredient of all."

"She must have asked you a million questions."

"Yes, she did, and I answered them all to her satisfaction."

I grabbed her around the waist and dragged her into the water. She screamed and pushed me away, running farther out into the ocean. The water was freezing, and her nipples popped right out through her suit. I grabbed her by her feet and spread her legs apart, sticking my foot right in her crotch.

"Do you love me?" I asked.

"No."

I pushed harder.

"Do you love me?"

"Yes, yes, cut it out!"

I let her feet go and pulled her toward me by the waist, trying to kiss her, as she resisted.

"You don't love me," I said.

"No, I don't," she said, and laughed.

I dragged her under the water and put my hand on her pussy. She kissed me, and I slid my hand under her suit.

"Not here," she said.

"Where then?"

"Not now."

"Let's walk back to the house, and I'll get my car," I said.

"We can't leave the others."

"Why not? They don't care."

"If we go back to the house, I want to pick up a newspaper and start looking for an apartment."

"That's fine," I said.

We got out of the water and the sun beat down on us. We told the others we were leaving and walked back to the house. There was no one around, so we went in our house and fucked our brains out. I came all over her face and felt satisfied. Nobody fucked like she did.

We drove my car to a local store and picked up a newspaper. Fortunately, we were not in a very expensive part of California, so the two bedrooms we were looking at were reasonable.

"I want to live by the beach," she said.

"So do I. How much can you afford?"

"I think my father will give me six or seven hundred for an apartment, and more for expenses."

"I can get about the same."

"We can get a nice place on the beach for that," she said.

"Yeah, I know of one in that complex right behind where we usually hang out."

"Oh, that's a nice building. Let's call and go look at it," she said.

"All right."

I remembered the name of the real estate agency and gave them a call. It turned out the apartment was vacant, and the owner was nearby. We agreed to meet him in an hour and began to get really excited. We both wanted desperately to get out of the halfway houses and start the semblance of a normal life. I made some coffee and put on some music. Laura smoked too, which I knew would make it easier when we lived together.

"How much do they want for the apartment?" she asked.

"Twelve hundred including heat."

"That's perfect."

"I know. Isn't it great?"

We sat outside, drinking our coffee and smoking. She was so beautiful when she was smiling and happy. I thought I had made the right decision. I thought about Linda for a second, but her face slipped out of my mind. I knew I would be able to let her go as long as I was with Laura.

"We have to leave in a little while. Do you want to change your clothes?" I asked.

"Yeah, I do. Give me a minute first."

"What do we do about the rehab? Just tell them we're leaving?" I asked.

"Of course. They can't keep us."

"I wonder if my mother will be okay with this," I said.

"My father will probably protest, but there's nothing he can do about it," she said.

"He can decide not to give you any money."

"He would never do that. I'm going to tell him that I'm going back to school and that I'm getting married. He's wanted that for me for a long time."

"I think I can get a teaching job around here. There are lots of colleges."

"Why don't you just write? You're always telling me you can't teach and write at the same time."

"Maybe I will; you'll inspire me."

She went next door to put on some clothes, and I took a quick shower. We got in my car and went to the apartment complex. The real estate agent was waiting for us, but the owner hadn't shown up yet. She took us inside, and we were thrilled with the apartment. The owner came by a few minutes later, and we signed a lease. I felt like my life had a new beginning.

"I'm so happy," she said as we drove back.

"Me too."

"What are we going to do about furniture and your paintings back in Syracuse?"

"I've thought about that. We'll buy some used furniture to start. We don't need much, and I'll store my paintings at my mother's."

"Do you have to fly back to straighten things out?"

"No, I think my mother and brother can do everything."

"Good, because I don't want you to leave my side for a minute."

When she said that, I began to panic. I needed a lot of space and enjoyed my solitude immensely. I knew she wasn't perfectly serious, but I was hoping she would find things to do. I hoped school would work out for her.

"Let's go to the beach and tell the guys about our apartment," she said.

We drove along the beach and spotted George's van not too far away. We walked down to them and sat in the blazing sun. The air was hot, but the water was still cold.

"Hey, we found an apartment," Laura said. "It's right there in that building, and it's facing the beach!"

"When are you guys moving out?" George said.

"Tomorrow," I said, "but I have to arrange everything with my mother."

"We're going to miss you," Jen said.

"We'll be around all the time," I said. "You guys can come over; we'll still be here."

"Another rehab marriage," George said, laughing, "but I know this one will work out."

"You're so pessimistic, George," Laura said.

"Realistic," he said.

"I could say something," Laura said, "but I'm not going to."

"I hope the best for you," George said. "I really do."

"We're not getting married right away, anyway. We know it takes time to adjust," I said.

The sun was slipping down slowly, and I thought that it had

been a great day. I was in love, and there is no better feeling. I wasn't thinking too far down the road; all I wanted to do was get out of the halfway house.

"Do you guys want to barbecue tonight?" I asked.

"Sure," George said.

"We'll make the salad," Jen said.

We went back to the houses and took showers. I called my mother, who wasn't too thrilled with my plan but agreed to wire me some money. I went over to see Laura, who had already talked to her parents.

"What did they say?" I asked.

"My father was reluctant, but he's sending me the money anyway."

"My mother was the same way."

"We have to go shopping for a bed and a couch tonight," she said.

"We need to call about phone service and get the lights turned on too," I said.

"I can't believe we're moving," she said. "I'm so excited."

"Yeah, no more restrictions on when we have to be home and when we can smoke inside," I said.

"We can fuck whenever we want to," she said.

We barbecued that evening, and it felt as if we were saying goodbye to our old friends. That night, I lay awake in my bed, excited for the future. It was a new beginning, and I was determined to make it work.

## Chapter Fourteen

We had put off shopping until the next day, and I only got two hours of sleep that night. Laura didn't sleep well either, but we still had lots of energy. I went for an early jog but didn't go too far. I showered and drove to Starbucks. Laura was already there with Jen and the guys.

"What's up, handsome?" Laura said, giving me a kiss.

"I called about the phone and the electricity," I said.

"We have to tell Steve we're leaving today," she said.

"We can do that as soon as we get back," I said. "We have a lot to do; let me get a coffee, and we'll get going."

The first thing we did was go to a furniture store. We bought a bed, couch, and coffee table. We paid on layaway, because we had good credit. They couldn't deliver until the next day, so we had to sleep on the rug that night. We bought a phone and some other things; we were having a lot of fun playing house.

"Let's go back to the rehab and tell Steve we're leaving," I said.

"Okay."

We drove back to the house and went directly to Steve's office. Our insurance was paying for our stay, so we expected an argument from Steve, the director. He wasn't busy when we arrived, and we went right in.

"We're leaving," I said simply.

"Together?" he said.

"Yup," she said.

"Are you sure that's a good idea? You were both planning on staying a few more months," he said.

"We're getting married, and we already have an apartment," I said.

"Suit yourselves," he said. "I'll have the paperwork drawn up."

"Thanks," I said.

As we left, I said to Laura, "That was easy enough."

"He's really a nice guy; this probably happens all the time," she said.

We went to the apartment and took a long nap. Then we made love. I was beginning to feel like a new man with a new life. She was so excited; she could hardly contain herself.

"Let's go to the beach, the guys will probably be there," I said.

"Let's see if we can see George's van from the window," she said.

Sure enough, there was the van, in the same spot. We put on our suits and flip flops and walked to the beach.

"Hey, there they are!" Eliot said.

"We haven't forgotten you," I said.

"We thought we'd never see you again," Jen said.

"You're still my closest buddy," Laura said to Jen.

"Yeah, but you know how that goes once somebody hooks up with a man," Jen said.

"We're all a team," I said.

We sat on the beach and got some rays. The islands stood majestically in the distance. It was a perfect day, and nothing was bothering me.

"What did Steve say?" Eliot asked.

"He was cool with everything," Laura said.

"I'm so glad you're not far away," Jen said.

"We still have to get dishes, and pots and pans," Laura said, "but we'll have you all over for lunch or dinner."

"Why don't you eat with us tonight?" George asked. "We'll go in the cafeteria; it'll only cost you a couple of bucks."

"Good idea," I said.

After an hour, Laura and I went back to the apartment. We were still excited with our new place.

"See if the phone works, will you, sweetheart?" I said, as I stepped in the shower.

"It works!" she said.

After we showered, we went over to the houses to see our friends. The three of them were hanging out at the picnic table. The sun was beginning to dip lower, and it was getting cool out. It was obvious that Eliot and Jen were getting closer all the time. They were sitting right next to each other, holding hands.

"There are the newlyweds," Eliot said.

"Maybe you two should get married," Laura said.

"Maybe we will," Jen said, looking at Eliot with a smile.

After an hour of chit-chatting, we went into the cafeteria to eat. The food was good, and I thought we would miss eating here. We had a few laughs; then we departed. Laura and I went to our apartment and organized some cushions we had borrowed to sleep that night. George had procured a television for us, so we watched that for a while.

"Jen said she wanted to talk to me tonight. I'm going over there for a while," Laura said.

"What time are you coming back?" I asked.

"In an hour or two; you can go to sleep if you want to."

She left and I went to sleep.

Two hours later I woke up, and Laura hadn't returned. I called Jen's house, but Jen said she hadn't seen her all night. I called Eliot, but she said he hadn't seen her either. Then it occurred to me to see if my car was still there. The car was gone, I started to panic, but there was nothing I could do. I called Eliot again, and he tried to calm me down.

"She probably went drinking," he said.

"I'm not so worried about that," I said. "I just don't want her in those bad neighborhoods; anything could happen."

"If you want, you can call the police and have them track down your car."

"I think I will, thanks. I might call you later," I said.

"Okay, but try to relax."

"Easier said than done."

I called the police, but they said I had to wait a day to report the car was stolen. Now I was really frustrated. I just had to wait. I was getting angry as well, but knew it was the disease I was angry at. Now all my dreams came crashing down.

At about two in the morning, Laura showed up. She was drunk as a skunk and laughing hysterically.

"Where have you been?" I yelled.

"I went to a little bar down the road. Don't worry, your car is safe," she slurred.

"Go to sleep," I said. "We'll talk about it in the morning; there's no sense talking now."

She passed out, but I couldn't get to sleep. The floor was so uncomfortable. I tried everything with the cushions I had, but nothing worked. At four in the morning, I took a hot bath and tried to relax. I was thinking of calling Eliot. I hesitated for a while; then I called him.

"It's me," I said.

"Did she come home yet?" he asked.

"Yeah, a couple of hours ago."

"Is she all right?"

"She passed out. I think she'll be fine. Now I don't know what I've got myself into."

"I told you that you were taking a big risk."

"I know; I remember only too well."

"You can't let her jeopardize your sobriety."

"You're right, but how can I kick her out? We both signed the lease?"

"Leases can be broken. But why don't you see how she acts? This may be a one-time thing."

"Good idea."

I tried getting to sleep, with no success. I was in a very bad mood when I finally decided to get up. I took a hot shower and had some coffee, trying to calm down. Laura didn't wake up until eleven, and she had a wicked hangover.

"Is there any coffee?" she said meekly.

"Yeah, sure, and take some aspirin."

"Please don't lecture me; I feel bad enough as it is."

"Maybe you need to go back to rehab," I said.

"No, I'll be all right. I was just celebrating my freedom."

"You can't do that."

"I know; I know."

"I'm not going to lecture you, but I can't live with you if you're going to drink."

"I know. I think I'll go to outpatient; that should keep me occupied for most of the day."

"Well, as soon as you get showered and dressed, we're going to a meeting."

"That's okay with me."

I made some phone calls to my family while she took a shower. I knew she wasn't feeling good, but I wasn't going to baby her. Now the cravings would kick in again, and the disease would take over. I hoped she would be able to get it under control, but I wasn't too optimistic. If she couldn't quit, I would have to move to a cheaper apartment or live with Eliot. Eliot and I were planning to live together anyway, so at least I had a way out. I wasn't too worried about the lease. There wasn't much the landlord could do.

When Laura was dressed, we went to a meeting in town, and I was glad to see a lot of my friends. I could tell Laura wasn't feeling well, so afterwards we went right home, and she went back to sleep. I called Eliot right away, but he was out. I looked out the window and saw George's van parked near the beach. I walked down there and found that Jen was with the boys.

"How you doing, little buddy?" Eliot said.

"Not too well," I answered.

"You guys left too early," George said.

"I know that now," I said sarcastically.

"It still might turn out all right," Eliot said. "You have to keep a close eye on her."

"I hate doing that; I'm not used to it. I should have stayed with Linda."

"Here we go again," George said.

I was really getting upset and thought about going home, but I changed my mind. I thought I would drag Jen into the conversation.

"What do you think, Jen?" I asked.

"I think if you really love her, like you say you do, you should stick by her. This might be a one-time thing; you don't know. I think you should forget about Linda, too."

"I can't. That's the problem."

"Did you call her and tell her you were engaged to Laura?" Eliot said.

"No. I keep putting if off."

"Well, don't call her now, or if you call her, don't say you're engaged," George said.

I thought about calling Linda and telling her I would take a quick trip back to Syracuse. I didn't think I could leave Laura alone now though, so I forgot about that. I would call her, but I didn't know what I would say to her. Somehow, I had to keep that relationship alive. I hadn't talked to her for a while. I would have to wait until Laura was gone or asleep.

"Why don't you guys come over for dinner?" I asked.

"We'll order pizza," George said.

"Eliot, maybe you can talk to Laura," I said.

"I'll talk to her," he said.

"She's got to go to three meetings a day for a while, until she gets the cravings out of her system," George said.

"This scares me," Jen said.

"You should be scared; we're all scared," Eliot said.

"I'm going to bring up fear as a topic at a meeting tonight," I said.

"Good idea," Eliot said. "Don't think for a minute that Laura isn't full of fear."

"I can't believe she went out on the first night," I said.

"Happens all the time," George said.

I wanted to go home and call Linda. She would be done with dinner at about this time, and Laura was probably still sleeping.

"I have to live with someone in recovery," Jen said. "I need the extra security."

"Maybe we could live together, the five of us, like a halfway house," Eliot said, laughing.

"Actually, that's not a bad idea," I said. "You know what they say; there's strength in numbers."

"I have a family," George said, "but maybe the four of you could get a duplex and keep an eye on each other."

"I'm going home, guys," I said.

"All right, we'll see you in a couple of hours," Eliot said.

I walked home, planning to call Linda if Laura was asleep. I was nervous about my own sobriety now. I knew Laura would take me back out before I got her sober again. I didn't want to use, but I knew that if I were around it, I would. Laura was still asleep when I got home, so I took the phone in the kitchen and called Linda.

"Hi, stranger," she said.

"Hi, yourself, beautiful."

"Did you get my messages?"

"Yeah, I got them. I've been busy getting an apartment for myself."

"You've got an apartment now?"

"Yup, and I'm staying with one of my friends; nobody you know; it's right on the beach."

"Oh, I want to come out there."

"Not right now, sweetheart, let me get settled in."

"All right, so why don't you come home for a week? I'm almost done with my studies."

"I was thinking about it, but there's so much for me to do around here first."

"Is there room for me if I came out there?"

"Sure, of course, there is."

I could feel myself getting in trouble the more I spoke, so I decided to end the conversation rather abruptly. I told her I had to run to a meeting, and that I would call her the next day. I could hear Laura in the bathroom not a minute later and wondered if she had heard any part of the conversation. I made some coffee and waited until Laura got out of the shower.

She came out into the kitchen in her bathrobe with a towel on her head.

"Who were you on the phone with?"

"My mother."

"Is everything all right?"

"Yeah, I was asking her for more money. Do you feel better now?"

"Much better. We should talk."

"Go ahead. I'm listening."

"I will never, I repeat, never, do that again."

"Don't make promises you can't keep."

"I can keep that promise, I assure you. I'm really sorry, Paul. I don't know what came over me."

"You're just a good alcoholic, that's all, like me."

"I want to be with you though, and I know I can't be with you if I drink."

"That's right, and if you drink, you might get into drugs again, and kill yourself."

"I'm going to go to two meetings a day, I promise, and never leave your side."

"Maybe we can do that for a while, but I have to be able to trust you."

"You will; you'll see."

"How do you feel by the way?"

"Much better."

"The guys are coming over for dinner. We're ordering

pizza."

We cleaned up the apartment a bit, and I called my father to check in with him. My brother didn't call as often, but the whole family was keeping a close eye on me. My father and I were very close, and he had a way of loosening me up. A couple of hours later, the crew showed up, and we ordered some pizza and soda. I took Eliot aside and reminded him to talk to Laura. He took Laura into the bedroom and talked to her until the food arrived.

When they came out, he told me he thought she would be all right. He said she was determined to stay sober and that the night before was an aberration. We enjoyed eating the pizza; it was like a party without the beer.

"Are you going to be all right, Laura?" Jen said.

"Yeah, I'll be fine. I have to learn how to celebrate without drinking. That's all."

"You, or we, I should say, have to learn everything all over again," Eliot said.

"I think we've got the fucking down to an art," I said with a laugh.

"I still feel awkward socializing," Jen said.

"I know what you mean," Laura said. "You're not quite sure if you've said the right thing."

"I feel pretty comfortable talking to you guys," George said, "but my wife is another thing altogether."

"That's why we have to practice with each other," Eliot said, "so that when we talk to normal people, they won't think we're weird."

"My family thinks I'm weird anyway," Laura said.

"When will it ever come naturally?" I said to Eliot.

"In a couple of years, depending on how fast you learn," he said.

"I'm glad I was sober in my twenties," I said. "That's when I really learned how to socialize."

"Why did you start smoking pot so late?" Jen said.

"I had a nervous breakdown, and I couldn't teach or study, so I started hanging out at this bar. The rest is history," I said.

"You must have smoked a lot of pot in just a few years," George said.

"I made up for lost time," I said.

"Getting back to normal should be easier for you," Eliot said.

"What's normal?" Laura said.

"Nobody's normal," Eliot said.

I was glad to have my new friends around me; I didn't know if I could make as good friends anywhere else. I was afraid to go back to Syracuse, back to that toxic environment. I felt safe in California. I didn't know anyone who dealt marijuana, and I had a lot of support.

"My mother's normal," I said with a laugh.

"I'm sure she is; you're lucky," Jen said.

That was the only drawback. I didn't know if I could live so far away from my family. My mother and I were so close, and she was my greatest support. My twin brother and I were very close too, as were my older brother and I.

"Well, I like being abnormal," Laura said. "It makes me feel unique."

"We're all unique anyway," Eliot said.

"Yeah, but some of us are more unique than others," Laura said, laughing.

"I wouldn't mind just fitting in," Jen said. "A lot of times I feel like a square peg in a round hole."

"You fit in with us fine," Eliot said, giving her a kiss on the forehead.

We finished eating, and the three of them left. Suddenly, I dreaded being left alone with Laura. Of course, I cared about her, but living with her was different. She was very needy, and frankly, I didn't want to take care of her.

"I'm exhausted," she said.

"I'm sure you are. Why don't you go to bed?"

"I think I will. What are you going to do?"

"I'm going to do some writing and maybe call my brothers."

"I have to call my sister and my mother later," she said.

She went to bed, and I sat down at the kitchen table we had just bought. The writing came easily, which surprised me, and I quickly finished.

# Chapter Fifteen

I went to bed exhausted, but Laura woke up. She wanted to make love, but all I wanted to do was go to sleep. I won. We slept well together, even though I got up a few times in the night. The second time I awoke, Laura got up with me and convinced me to fuck her brains out. I got horny as soon as she began to rub my cock. She was so sexy with her smooth skin and long legs.

I rolled her on her stomach and licked her pussy from behind. She got wet in a couple of seconds and started talking.

"Fuck me, Paul, fuck me. I want you to stick that big cock of yours inside me."

She was up on her knees, and I penetrated her quickly. It went right in. I fucked her and fucked her until I was ready to come. She turned around swiftly, and I squirted my come in her mouth. After I came, she masturbated herself for a minute, until she came too. Afterwards, we were exhausted and fell right to sleep.

In the morning, I had a dream that I was using cocaine with Laura on the beach, and Eliot walked up to us. It was a terrible dream, and I woke up sweating.

The sun was streaming through the windows, and I felt much better being awake. I was getting more sleep now and didn't feel as anxious during the day.

"Good morning, sweetheart," she said.

"Good morning. I just had the worst nightmare."

"Oh, I'm sorry. Do you want to tell me about it?"

"Not really."

"I'm hungry," she said.

"Let's call the guys and go out for breakfast," I said.

"Good idea."

We showered and called Eliot and George. Eliot answered.

"Hey, what's up?" he said.

"We want to go out and eat."

"Why don't you come over here? We've got eggs, bacon, and potatoes."

"Deal."

We decided to walk over to the house, since the weather was so nice. I held Laura's hand as I did once in a while. I was thinking that if we could both stay sober, this could work.

"I need to go to a meeting," Laura said.

"I do, too. But what's the matter?"

"I've been thinking about drinking and using again."

"Maybe we should skip breakfast and go to that early meeting on the beach," I said.

"That would be nice, but we'd have to go back and get the car."

"Okay with me. I'll call Eliot again and cancel."

We walked back to the apartment, and I called Eliot.

"Why don't I go with you; Jen might want to go too. George is going to spend time with his wife," Eliot said.

"That'll be great. We'll all go. I'll pick you up in a few minutes," I said.

It disturbed me that Laura was being tortured again by cravings. It was a mental obsession, as well as a physical one, and it would take several months for her to feel better. I hoped she had learned her lesson, but I knew I would have to keep a close eye on her.

"Let me put on a dress," Laura said. "I hope Jen goes."

"She and Eliot are becoming pretty close," I said.

"Maybe they'll get married," Laura said.

"I don't know about that. Eliot's already been married twice, and she's brand new to sobriety."

"Yeah, but look at us."

"Anything's possible, I guess."

We changed and got in the car. It was so nice to have a vehicle and have the days to ourselves. The sun was above the horizon, reflecting off the water. If only my emotions had been as calm as the view. We picked up Eliot and Jen and went to our meeting. Laura talked for a long time, which I was glad of, and she seemed to feel a lot better afterwards.

"Let's go home and eat," Eliot said.

"You've got to lose some weight," Jen said. "No potatoes for you."

We went back to Eliot's house and cooked a big breakfast. Laura and Jen got into this big conversation about recovery, and one would think they actually knew what they were talking about.

"You have to put the urge right out of your mind, as soon as it comes in," Laura said.

"And you have to avoid all the people who are drinking," Jen said.

"You have to avoid all negative people, whether they're drinking or not," Laura said.

"People, places, and things," Jen said.

I wanted to interject, but figured I was better off keeping my mouth shut. They talked for about half an hour, and I was glad they were talking about recovery. I felt relieved for the first time in two days, thinking that maybe Laura could stay sober. After breakfast, we all piled into the Cadillac and went to the beach. It was a hot day, and there were more people than usual lying in the sun.

"I feel great today," Laura said.

"Remember that feeling when you get sad again," Eliot said.

"Why do I have so many mood swings?" Laura asked Eliot.

"We all do in early recovery, but it's essential that we get out of this stage and start to accumulate some time," he said.

"I wish I hadn't gotten drunk," she said.

"Don't beat yourself up over it. Move on, and don't do it again," he said.

"I'm resolved," she said.

We lay out in the sun, and I noticed Laura was getting a pretty good tan, making her sexier than ever. I rubbed lotion all over her body and made a few lewd comments. Laura and I were very playful with our language. We didn't get offended easily. I was getting horny watching her and was impatient to take her home and fuck her. Jen and Eliot went into the water, and I noticed they were fooling around under the surf.

"You forgive me for taking your car and going out the night before last, don't you, Paul?"

"Of course, I forgive you. Just don't do it again," I said.

"I won't. You're so good to me," she said in a soft voice.

I wanted to smoke a joint in the worst way, but rapidly put it out of my mind. I watched the seagulls flying around and reminded myself of my newfound freedom.

"I want to fuck you," I said to her.

"I'm up for that. Do you want to do it in the water?"

"Sure."

We waded out a little ways, but the water was freezing, and

my cock shriveled right up. I looked over to Eliot and Jen, who seemed to be having a lot of fun.

"Oh, my God, it's freezing!" Laura said.

"I know it; I don't know if I can get it up."

"I'll help you; don't worry."

We went out until the water was shoulder-high and hugged each other. She grabbed my cock under my suit, and soon I was hard. She removed her bottoms and climbed up on me. I had a lot of trouble putting it in, and the water kept her from getting lubricated. We fucked for a few minutes, while Eliot made comments, but it didn't feel that good. We laughed and laughed, and decided to try again later.

"It's freezing. Let's get out," I said.

We walked to the shore and met Eliot and Jen on the beach.

"That was fun," Jen said. "Did you see that couple staring at us?" she said with a laugh.

"They're jealous," Eliot said.

"It's a good thing this beach isn't crowded," Laura said.

"I could smoke a joint right about now," I said.

"Where did that come from?" Laura said. "You have to be the strong one."

"I was just kidding," I said.

"No, you weren't," Eliot said.

"I was, but I wasn't," I said. "Where do these strong cravings come from? Right out of the blue!"

"You have to put them out of your mind as soon as they come in," Jen said.

"That's right," Eliot said.

"I should never have gone out the other night," Laura said. "Now my cravings are worse than ever."

"It's a progressive disease," Eliot said. "If you pick up again, it's like you never stopped."

"I hope George is all right," I said.

"He'll be fine," Jen said.

It was time to go, so we packed up our things and rode out. On the ride back, I kept thinking that I wished I still lived in the halfway house. We dropped Eliot and Jen off, then went home. There was nothing to do, so I turned on the television and watched the news.

"I'm going to make some coffee. Do you want some?" Laura said.

"No thank you, but I'll have a coke."

I decided to call George just to check up on him.

"Hey, what's up?" I said.

"My wife is drunk, and we're having a fight."

"Why don't you leave?"

"I think I'm going to."

I could hear his wife screaming in the background. I hung up the phone and told Laura about it.

"I don't know how they'll ever be able to get back together again," she said.

"I don't either."

"The kids must be really suffering," she said.

"The oldest boy has already run away several times," I said.

"Why doesn't she want to go for help while he is?" she said.

"Some people aren't ready, that's all. It's a scary proposition," I said.

"Maybe you should go over to the halfway house and talk to him," she said.

"Eliot will talk to him," I said.

I would have gone over, but I didn't want to leave Laura alone. I didn't trust myself, let alone her. I was already missing the freedom I had experienced before. I was not used to being tied down to somebody else, much less somebody I couldn't trust.

"Maybe we can go over together," I said.

"I take it you don't want to leave me alone."

"Well..."

"You don't have to say it. It's written all over your face."

"Don't be upset, honey, but I can't trust you yet; we'll have to wait a couple of months."

"How is that going to work? You have to stay by my side everywhere I go?"

"Pretty much, I guess."

"That's ridiculous. I need my freedom," she said.

"Come on, let's go to the halfway house," I said.

"I'll go with you now, but you had better rethink being stuck to my side."

"It'll be all right. You'll see."

We walked to the house and found Eliot eating cookies in front of the television. George hadn't arrived yet.

"What's up, guys?" Eliot said.

"We came over to console George," I said. "He had a fight with his wife."

"Is she drunk?" he said.

"Yup," Laura said.

Eliot put on a pot of coffee, and we ate some cookies. I wished I still lived there. Eliot was very comforting like an older brother. Eliot picked up some of the clothes in the living room. The house needed to be cleaned. We were all coffee junkies, but we figured it was better than anything else. George showed up a few minutes later.

"I can't believe that bitch!" he said.

"She's not a bitch," Eliot said calmly.

"What do you know about it?" George said.

"Calm down," I said.

"I feel like getting fucked up," George said.

"What were you arguing about?" Eliot said.

"Nothing, absolutely nothing. She's pissed off because the kids aren't behaving, and I'm supposed to be there. Well, how can I be there right now? She keeps getting drunk and doesn't want to get help. Of course, the kids aren't behaving!"

"You have to put yourself in her shoes; she's only thirty years old and probably won't seek recovery until she turns forty, if ever, so you have to see that. She's at her wit's end in the house all by herself," Eliot said.

"I know, I know, but I'm at my wit's end too; she doesn't know what I'm going through in early recovery. All she sees is that I'm going to the beach every day; she doesn't know about the turmoil in my mind."

I was glad I wasn't in his position; though I had a great deal of empathy and sympathy. Laura was perfectly quiet. She was smart to stay out of it. I had never seen George so wound up. We were drinking a lot of coffee, and it occurred to me that I would have difficulty sleeping that night.

"Of course, she's upset. The beach seems a lot better than staying home with three wild kids," Eliot said. "Calm down now. Let's end this conversation."

"I wish she weren't drinking. She'd be able to handle her problems a lot better," George said.

Finally, Laura spoke up.

"Maybe she'll follow your lead; she might see that she needs a vacation too," she said.

"It's hardly a vacation," I said.

We all quieted down, and I heard George take a deep breath. It was getting late, so Laura and I decided to go home. We hopped in the car and drove along the beach for a while before we headed home.

"I'll never drink again," Laura said.

"I hope not," I said. "I think together we can stay sober, but we have to surround ourselves with a sober network."

"I obsessed over it for a couple of hours," she said. "That's all it takes."

"At least you didn't do cocaine," I said.

"I'm more determined than ever," she said.

When we got home, I was too tired to have sex, but she really wanted to. I told her I would satisfy her in the middle of the night, after I got some rest.

## Chapter Sixteen

I did wake up in the middle of the night, but she was sound asleep, so I didn't disturb her. I walked out to the balcony and watched the moon reflect off the ocean. I often thought about philosophy at these moments, and it simply occurred to me how much more optimistic Derrida sounded in comparison to de Man. I was trying to stay away from these thoughts; they only made me manic.

As I was sitting out on the balcony, I heard Laura in the kitchen. A few minutes later, she brought me a cup of tea.

"Just think how much more we appreciate nature when we're sober," I said.

"I didn't appreciate anything when I was high," she said.

"Sometimes, I wish I believed in God," I said.

"You can if you want to," she said.

"It's not that simple."

"Look at the moon," she said.

"Beautiful like you," I said.

"For an atheist, you're quite the Romantic," she said.

"It's the Italian in me."

"You must have been raised Catholic."

"Yes, I was."

"What happened?"

"I got disillusioned."

"Me too," she said.

We drank our tea quietly, and simply started at the ocean. I knew she wanted to make love, but for once I wasn't in the mood. I was beginning to think that our relationship could work, or at least I was hopeful. I thought about Linda; I would have to call her and tell her about Laura.

"Do you want some cookies? Eliot gave me some," she said.

"Sure. Why not?"

After an hour of being up and chit-chatting, we went back to bed. She started rubbing my cock, and soon I had an erection. I didn't want to go through all the foreplay, so I stuck it in and fucked her hard. I made her come, but didn't come myself. I slept well after that and didn't wake up until eight o'clock, which was late for me.

When I got up, she was cleaning the kitchen and waiting to make me breakfast.

"How do you feel?" she said.

"I feel great. How about you?"

"I feel good too. Does your medication make you groggy in the morning?"

"A little bit, but after a cup of coffee, I'm wide awake," I said.

"It doesn't affect your erections," she said.

"But it makes it harder for me to ejaculate," I said.

"Why don't we call George and Eliot and Jen to see what they're up to," she said.

"They're probably at Starbucks already," I said. "I'll call."

When I called, Eliot answered.

"Hey, what's up?" I said.

"Do you guys want to go up to Santa Barbara with me?" he asked.

"Sure. We can go in my car," I said.

"Be here in an hour," he said.

After I hung up, I was all excited.

"We're going to Santa Barbara," I said.

"Oh great, I can wear my new sundress," Laura said.

"We'll probably go to the nude beach."

"Oh, I hate that place," she said. "There are a bunch of dirty old men along the wall, getting off on the young chicks."

"Like me?" I said, laughing.

"You know what I mean. If we go there, Jen and I are staying in the car."

"Well, then, we won't go there."

We ate breakfast and got dressed for our trip. The car was low on gas, so we stopped at the station. The three of them had made food for a picnic, and luckily everybody was in a good mood.

The drive along the coast was spectacular, and traffic was light. The sun was rainy and reflecting off the ocean. I thought that if every day could be like this, I would be a happy man.

"I want to go to the nude beach," Jen said.

"We already had this discussion," I said.

"And what did you decide?" Jen said.

"Oh, it's horrible, Jen," Laura said. "There are all these dirty old men there."

"I like dirty old men," she said laughingly at Eliot.

"Well, you can go, but I'm not," Laura said.

"We'll go another time," I said.

George was particularly quiet. I was wondering what he was thinking.

"Hey, George," I said, "do you want to go that little café in the middle of town, for lunch?"

"Yeah, I'd like to," he said.

"You're going to stay in a good mood, aren't you, buddy?" I

said.

"I hope so," he said.

"Did you talk to your wife this morning?" I asked.

"Yes, for a little while; we both apologized, which made me feel better," he said.

The car seemed to glide over the road. I looked at all the houses along the beach and wished I owned one. We were getting close, and traffic was getting heavier. Some days in early recovery seemed perfect.

"How often do you fight and then apologize?" Laura said.

"Quite often these days," George said.

"You've got to get past that stage," Jen said, "though obviously I'm no expert."

"He hit you, then apologized?" Eliot said.

"Pretty much," Jen said.

"What a bastard!" Eliot said, giving Jen a kiss on the cheek.

We finally arrived in Santa Barbara and drove down the main drag.

Everybody was outside, walking and sitting in the various restaurants. The women were all wearing shorts or short skirts.

"That's the place," George shouted.

"There's no parking," I said.

"We have to find a side street," Laura said.

I drove around for a while, until we found a parking spot. We got out and walked to the main street. I was surprised at how crowded it was. We found the café and had to wait half an hour to get a seat outside. We didn't mind waiting, but George seemed a little anxious. After we sat down, we ordered our coffee and talked lightly about the weather and various topics. Suddenly, Eliot asked us all to be quiet.

"Jen, will you marry me?" he said, while everybody looked

on in shock.

"Don't put me on the spot, honey."

"I'll understand if you don't want to, or if you need time to think about it," he said.

"I need time," she said.

We all breathed a deep sigh of relief. Then we all laughed.

"At least I didn't get rejected right off the bat," Eliot said.

"I will marry you," Jen said.

"I thought you needed time," Eliot said.

"I really love you; I don't need more time," she said.

"Well, then, it's time to celebrate," Eliot said. He raised his ice latte in the air and said, "May God bless these three couples."

"I guess it's better that it's coffee instead of champagne," George said with a laugh.

Jen and Eliot kissed each other lightly and sat back down. Some other people had heard what was going on and applauded.

"I'm the happiest man in the world," Eliot said.

"We're all happy for you too," I said.

"Let's not set a date yet, though," Jen said.

"Maybe in a year or two we can have a double ceremony," Laura said.

"I can't wait a year or two; well, perhaps a year," Eliot said.

"Let's discuss this in private," Jen said.

We changed the subject and talked about all kinds of different things. George loosened up after a while and joined in. After we had our coffees, we walked up and down the main street, looking at all the windows. Laura had expensive tastes and, at one point, we came to a jewelry store.

"I want a diamond like that one," Laura pointed.

"Are you going to buy it?" I asked.

"No, you're going to buy it for me," she said; then she

laughed.

"How about that one?" I said, pointing to a much smaller one.

"Is that all you love me?" she said.

"If I could afford it, I'd buy you the Hope diamond," I said with a laugh.

After our walk, we got back in the car and drove back to Oxnard. The sun was above the water, reflecting nicely off the ocean. Eliot couldn't stop talking. He was like a little kid.

"Are there any more apartments in your complex?" he said to me.

"I think there is one," I said.

"Or, maybe I'll build our own house!" he said.

"Calm down, honey," Jen said.

"I can't calm down; I'm so excited," he said.

Laura had a big grin on her face, but George was rather quiet.

"Do you want to have children?" Eliot said to Jen.

"Hush now," she said.

"All right, I'll be quiet, but it's under protest," he said.

The drive back seemed quicker than the drive there. We pulled into the school at about dinner time and dropped our friends off. Laura and I drove along the beach for a while, before going home. There wasn't much in the refrigerator, but we managed to pull a salad together. After dinner, we relaxed in front of the television and ate nachos.

"I'm bored; I'm going for a walk," Laura said.

"No, you're not," I said.

"What do you mean, I'm not? The sun is setting over the ocean. I'm not going to just sit in front of the T.V."

"I don't feel like going for a walk; we walked all day," I said.

"I'm not going to drink. I simply want to be outside!"

"Tomorrow."

"No, I'm going now; you can't control every move that I make!"

"All right, go, but it you come home drunk, I won't be here tomorrow."

"Fine!"

She stormed out of the house, and I noticed she forgot her key. I thought maybe I should follow her, but I didn't. I was having a lot of trouble with this control issue, and now I only wanted to be free of the relationship. I sat in front of the television but didn't even notice what the movie was. I felt angry, and I hated that feeling. All kinds of things were running through my mind, including what I would do the next day if she came home drunk. I decided to call Eliot.

"Hey, what's up?" he said.

"Laura went for a walk, and I'm worried she's going to get drunk."

"Why didn't you go with her?"

"I don't want to follow her around everywhere she goes."

"Then leave it alone."

"I told her I'd be gone tomorrow if she came home drunk."

"Well, now she knows; she'll be all right; it's a good evening to take a walk."

"We had a mini fight before she left."

"Let it go."

"I can't; I'm really upset."

"How do you think she feels?"

"Yeah, I guess you're right."

"Go find her."

"Okay, bye."

I got dressed and went out to look for her. I didn't have to go far. She was sitting on the beach in front of the apartment. The sun had set, and it was getting pretty chilly out. She had forgotten her jacket and was shivering in the evening air.

"Hey, how are you?" I said.

"Mad."

"I know. I'm sorry, I really am. I guess I don't trust you yet," I said.

"I can understand that; I haven't been the perfect model of sobriety, but you're going to have to trust me, at least a little, sooner or later," she said.

"I know, I know. But why don't we make it a little later? I'll tell you what. Why don't we stay close together for a month? Then you can have your freedom, and I can have mine."

"You mean I have to go another month without a car?"

"Is that acceptable? I'll take you anywhere you want to go. It's for your own good."

"I guess so."

"Don't stay mad. I'm really sorry," I said.

"I'm not mad any more."

"I love you," I said.

"I love you too."

"Do you want to go home and make love?" I asked.

"I thought you were too tired."

"I think I can muster up the energy."

We walked home slowly, hand in hand, and made love passionately for an hour. I tried taking a Viagra and was able to come twice, which I hadn't done in a long time. She spit it out the first time. She said it tasted too salty. I laughed when she spat out, and she slapped my ass.

"Don't laugh at me!" she said.

"I'm sorry; I couldn't help it."

"I should tan your hide."

"I like it. Do it again."

She smacked me again, and I burst out laughing. I liked it when we were playful this way. They were our best moments. I was exhausted afterwards and went right to sleep. Laura stayed up for a while and watched TV.

# Chapter Seventeen

I awakened twice during the night and remembered how I used to smoke pot at these times. Fortunately, both times I went right back to sleep. Laura rolled over and rarely woke up when I did. In the morning, I felt pretty refreshed and made a pot of coffee. Laura stayed in bed a while longer, so I walked outside to get the paper. When I returned, she was sitting in the kitchen in her underwear, looking sexy as hell.

"How did you sleep?" I asked.

"Pretty soundly. How about you?"

"Not bad."

"Why don't you give Eliot a call and see what they're up to," she said.

"Good idea, but they might have gone to Starbucks already."

I called Eliot, and they were still home.

"The three of us are going to the coffee shop in half an hour. Do you want to join us?" he said.

"Sure."

I told Laura she had to get ready right away.

"Let's shower together," she said.

"No fucking though," I said. "We really have to go."

When we got to Starbucks, the three of them were already there. Jen looked like she was all upset about something.

"I just had a panic attack," she told us.

"She's a little better now," Eliot said.

"Are you taking something for it?" Laura asked. "There are

anti-anxiety medicines."

"This was my first one," Jen said. "I'll have to talk to the doctor; it really freaked me out."

"What were you doing?" I asked.

"Nothing; I was only ordering my coffee."

"They can happen for no reason at all," Eliot said. "It's a chemical thing."

"Well, they'd better stop. I'll take medication or do yoga, but I'm not putting up with this," she said.

"I think you need more sex," Eliot said.

"It's not funny," Jen said.

We got our coffees and sat with them. Jen was calming down. George hadn't said a word since we got there. He had a way of observing things from a detached point of view. I was wondering if he had spoken to his wife that morning.

"Have you ever had a panic attack?" Jen asked Laura.

"Not exactly, but I've felt a lot of anxiety before."

"They're awful," Jen said.

"Why don't we take you to the doctor now?" George said. "He can give you a prescription today."

"Good idea," Jen said.

"We'll meet you at the beach later," I said.

The three of them took off in George's old Mercedes. Laura and I didn't say anything for a few minutes. I was wondering if we were already getting bored with each other. I could tell that Laura wasn't as comfortable being sober as I was. I had spent most of my twenties being sober, so I felt I was going back to a previous state. She hadn't been sober since she was thirteen.

"I hope that medication works for Jen," Laura said.

"It probably will."

"Did you ever feel a high level of anxiety?" Laura said.

"Recently I have."

"Oh, thanks a lot."

"That's not what I meant. It's hard for me to adjust too!"

"I know. Why is it so difficult?"

"Because we've been out of reality so long. Simple reality is a tough thing to take when you're not used to it."

"I don't think I like reality," she said.

"It's like hitting a brick wall at first; we'll get used to it. That's why we have to go to a lot of meetings."

"I don't understand how the meetings work either, though they definitely do."

"They provide enough relief for that day," I said, "but we have to do them on a daily basis. When you're quiet for an hour and talk for a few minutes, you calm down and focus on staying sober. It's like magic."

"I'm not like you," Laura said, "I'm afraid to talk. I always say, 'I'm glad to be here.'"

"You'll get over that; start to add a little bit every day. Tonight, try to think of reasons why you're grateful to be sober; you tell them to me all the time."

"I really am grateful, and you're the primary reason."

"You're clear-headed; you can make better decisions, stay out of trouble, get closer to your family; there are lots of reasons," I said.

"I should talk about my family more; they have supported me all along."

"They enabled you too," I reminded her.

We finished our coffee and went home. I wanted to make love to her after our intimate conversation, but we were expected at the beach. We packed up a few things and walked to our usual spot. The others weren't there yet, so we spread our blanket and stretched out. I was thinking that the reason I got into the pot to begin with was that I had too much time on my hands. I could have painted and written without it, but it hadn't been that way. Now was my chance to reforge my life.

"Here they come," I said, spotting the Mercedes in the distance.

"I wonder if Jen is with them," she said.

They pulled up, and Jen was with them. She seemed a lot better.

"How do you feel?" Laura said to Jen.

"I'm back to normal. The doctor prescribed me some medication and gave me free samples. I already took a pill."

"What did he say?" I asked.

"He said it isn't uncommon in early sobriety to encounter a lot of anxiety."

"How effective are the pills?" Laura said.

"He said they work wonders."

"She'll be fine," Eliot said.

Jen gave Eliot a big kiss and said, "I don't know what I'd do without you guys."

I winked at Laura and got up to go in the water. She followed me into the ocean, and we waded out until we were up to our shoulders. I pulled my suit down and put her hand on my cock. Then I slipped off her bottoms and put two fingers in her pussy. George shouted something from the beach, but I couldn't make it out. I saw Eliot and Jen walking toward us.

"Don't rub so hard," I said to Laura, who had a vicious grip on my cock.

"I'm sorry, sweetheart, but you're getting me so excited, I can't pay attention."

Eliot and Jen got near us and took off their suits as well. Jen turned away from Eliot, and I could see he was trying to enter her. He was having trouble though, and I started laughing.

"What are you laughing about?" he said.

"You!"

"The water is too cold," he said, laughing.

"Try pushing her head under water," I said.

Laura started laughing uncontrollably. We put our suits back on and walked to the beach. The sun felt good on my body, and all I wanted to do now was relax and slow down my thoughts. Eliot and Jen joined us, and George got a good laugh out of it all.

## Chapter Eighteen

After a couple of hours, Laura and I walked home, leaving the other three on the beach. I felt good, but my thoughts were still racing. I figured Laura was feeling pretty much the same.

"I think we need a meeting," I said, as I unlocked the door to our apartment.

"I know I do," she said.

"We can go to the hall. One's about to start in a little while."

We showered quickly, got dressed, and drove to the hall. A lot of people were standing outside smoking, and we joined them for a cigarette. Laura didn't smoke; she stood by my side and tried to chit chat. After a while, the meeting started, and we sat down in a fairly large group. The meeting began with some readings, and then we went around the room, sharing our experience, strength, and hope.

When it was Laura's turn, she said, "I'm really grateful to be here. I don't know what I would do without these meetings. I wouldn't have been able to meet Paul if I weren't sober, and I'm much closer to my family."

I patted her on the knee, signaling that she had done a good job. Then it was my turn to share.

"I'm really grateful to be sober these days. It's been a bit of a struggle. I've only been sober a couple of months. My sense of humor has returned, and that has been my biggest blessing. When somebody pushes my buttons, I turn it around and use self-deprecating humor. I can make fun of myself, laugh at myself, and gently tease others. I talk to my whole family every day, and Laura and I are planning on getting married!"

Everybody cheered, and I felt really happy. Laura gave me a kiss on the cheek and patted me on the back. After the meeting, Laura and I went to Starbucks for more coffee.

"I've never felt this way after a meeting," I said.

"You had really good things to say, and everybody liked what you said."

"You said some good things too; I'm proud of you for speaking more."

We sat at a table outside, and I was surprised it was so crowded in the evening.

"I'm getting addicted to those meetings," I said. "They really work."

"I'm starting to feel strongly about them too. There's a big speaker meeting in Malibu this Saturday. Can we go?" she said.

"Sure, that'll be great; there will be some stars there."

"Oh good! Maybe the others will come with us."

I was a little worried that I was drinking too much coffee. I didn't want to be awake half the night.

"Do you want to read that book they gave us, tonight?" she said.

"That's a good idea. I've already skimmed it. There are some interesting ideas in there."

"I need to go back to school," she said.

"Don't worry about that now; concentrate on being sober for a while; the other stuff will come later," I said.

"How long is it going to take us before we feel well enough to function?"

"It's hard to say; some never function again; others manage right away."

After our coffee, we got in the car and headed home. We drove along the beach for a while, as usual, and I felt really good. We were hungry. I was wondering what food we had in the refrigerator. When we got home, we noticed we didn't have much food, so we ordered a pizza.

"I hope Jen's all right," Laura said.

"I'm sure she's feeling better."

"Are there any messages on the machine?"

"No," I said.

"Let's call Eliot and George."

"All right."

I called Eliot, and George answered.

"Hey, what's up?" I said.

"My wife and I got into another fight," George said.

"Again?"

It's becoming a regular thing," he said.

"What was it about this time?"

"The kids, as usual."

"I'm sorry."

"She called me a fucking asshole."

"She didn't mean it," I said.

"But I feel like an asshole."

"Don't worry about it."

"Easy for you to say."

"Try to relax and take it easy for the rest of the night."

"I'll try. Do you want to talk to Eliot?"

"Yeah, put him on."

"Hey, what's up?" Eliot said.

"How's Jen feeling?" I asked.

"Much better, thanks; I think that medication really works. What are you guys up to?"

"We're going to do some reading together."

"And some fucking," Eliot said.

"Maybe."

I loved talking to Eliot; he made light of everything and put me at ease. He was more mature than the rest of us, but he could also act like a little kid; he had never lost his sense of humor.

"What chapter are you on?" he asked.

"We're going to start at the beginning. Laura hasn't read any of it yet."

"The doctor's opinion is very good," he said. "They finally recognized alcoholism as a disease, and that seriously changed the perspective on everything."

"Isn't that when they started building rehabs?"

"Well, that was much later; it took the community of physicians a long time to accept it as a disease."

"Listen. I'll call you in the morning. We'll go to the beach again tomorrow," I said.

When I got off the phone, I noticed that Laura had put on her negligee. She had a nice tan and looked great. I wanted to fuck her right then, but decided to do some reading instead. I read the first chapter to her while she rubbed my feet. We both found it interesting, so I kept reading.

"That's enough," she said, after I finished the second chapter.

"Let's take a bath together," I said.

"I'll draw the water."

We took a bath, and I fucked her while she was on her knees. I loved fucking her from behind. It had been a long day, and I was ready to go to sleep. I slept pretty well, but had a lot of negative dreams. They said in the meetings that my nightmares would go away after a few months. In the morning, I felt pretty refreshed and went for a walk along the beach before Laura got up. The sun was still hiding behind the hills, and the water was almost perfectly calm. I felt optimistic and reflected that I was born an optimist; I had little choice about it. After a while, I ran into Jen, who was walking the other way.

"Hey kiddo, what's up?" I said.

"Well, the doctor said a little exercise would go a long way in reducing my stress, so that's what I'm doing."

"I'm not really getting much exercise," I said. "I'm walking too slowly, but it's so relaxing."

"Did you talk to Eliot this morning?" she said.

"No. Why?"

"I was just wondering."

"Why don't you come over to our house, and we'll call him."

"Good idea."

We strolled leisurely to the apartment, and Laura was really glad to see Jen.

"Hey girl, how are you feeling?"

"Much better. That medication works well."

"Maybe it's that love feeling that is working so well," Laura said, winking at me.

"Eliot really is a great guy," Jen said.

"He's the best," I said.

I got on the phone, and George answered. He informed me that they were going to the coffee shop in a few minutes, so I told him we would meet him there.

"Get ready, Laura, we're going to meet the boys at Starbucks."

"I'm going to wear a hot skirt," Laura said.

"You're going to make me look bad," Jen said.

"You always look good," I said.

When Laura was ready, we got in the car and drove to the café. I was having a slight problem with the car, but I wasn't going to worry about it that morning. George and Eliot ware already there when we arrived. We got in line and waited patiently for our coffee. As we got to the front of the line, Jen started having a panic attack. She couldn't breathe; her eyes got wider, and she held her chest. Laura took her outside, and I ordered the coffee, pretending nothing was happening. I watched through the window as Jen sat down and reached into her purse for her medication. I knew the meds didn't work that way, but I figured they would make her feel better.

When I got outside, Jen was breathing easier, and the worst of it seemed to have passed.

"Why does it happen to me here?" she said.

"The memory of the last one may have triggered it," Eliot said.

"But I took my medication this morning," Jen said, exasperated.

"It may take longer to kick in," Eliot said. "Meds sometimes take a few weeks to start working. We'll talk to the doctor again when we get back."

Even though everybody was pretty excited, I felt calm and sipped my coffee. I was worried about Jen, but it didn't seem to bother me at the moment.

"Are you going to be all right?" I said to Jen.

"Yeah, I'm fine now; it comes so quickly, but then it seems to pass quickly too."

"Maybe we should take you back," George said.

"Let me sit for a minute," Jen said.

"Here, have some coffee," Laura said.

"Maybe it's the coffee that's giving me anxiety," Jen said.

"It could be," Eliot said.

"Yeah, I think I'll pass on the coffee right now until I ask the doctor."

After a few minutes, we got in our cars and went back home. There was a strong breeze that day, and it felt good. It wasn't so hot. I wanted to go to the beach, but Laura wanted to go shopping for things for the apartment. I would have bought her a car, but I didn't trust her. We went shopping and ended up getting a pair of matching lamps. We didn't have unlimited funds, so we had to budget carefully. When we got home, we called Jen to see how she was doing.

"Hey, you guys, thanks for calling," she said.

"We're worried about you," I said. "What did the doctor have to say?"

"He said the medication hasn't kicked in yet and that something or somebody at Starbucks triggered my reaction. He also said to cut down on the amount of caffeine I drink."

"Pretty much what we suspected," I said.

"Are you going to the beach this afternoon?" Jen asked.

"Sure, of course."

"I'm going to call Eliot; we'll meet you there," she said.

Laura and I took a short nap. Then we made love. Lovemaking was still exciting between us; we always tried to do new things. She had more energy than I, but I always managed to make her come. Sometimes, she had multiple orgasms, and I loved to watch her masturbate. After our shower, we walked to the beach and lay in the sun, until the others arrived. George was very upset when he got there.

"My wife wants a divorce," he said.

"She's going through a rough time right now; she doesn't mean it," I said.

"She's got a lawyer and everything," he said.

"You'd better get a lawyer too then," Eliot said.

"But I don't want a divorce," George said, almost crying.

"You may not have a choice," Eliot said.

"Here I am, getting sober and straightening out my life, while my world falls apart. I just want to get high!"

"Don't do that," Jen said.

"We're all having problems," Laura said. "If the Lord wants you to get divorced, then that's what it'll be."

We were all silent for a while, and George held his head in his hands. The sun was beginning to get hot. All I wanted to do was go in the water. The Santa Anna winds from the south were very strong, but it was still hot out.

"I'm going to go home and talk to her again," George said.

"Leave her alone now; you've got nothing to gain by that," Eliot said.

"I feel so helpless," George said.

"Maybe if you went to a meeting, you could take your mind off your problems," Jen said.

"That's a good idea," Laura said. "You could get feedback from the group."

"I hate those meetings," George said.

"You haven't always had that attitude," Eliot said.

"I'm going in the water," I said.

"Wait, Paul," Laura said.

"I'm sweating to death," I whined.

I was having trouble listening to other people's problems. I felt I had enough of my own. I didn't know how therapists held onto their sanity.

"Go ahead, Paul. I'm all right," George said.

"Come with me," I said to him.

"I'll go with you," Laura said. "Come on, George."

The three of us went in the water, while Eliot and Jen stayed on the beach. The ocean was cold, but it felt refreshing. George just stood in the water, staring out at the islands. I felt so sorry for him. I wasn't as close to George as I was to Eliot, but I still loved him.

"Swim a little!" I yelled to George.

After standing there for a while, he finally dove in. Then he swam far out, and I started to worry about him. He was a strong swimmer, but it was dangerous nonetheless. I yelled at him, and he came back; I didn't want him to try anything foolish. I went under the water and swam over to Laura, biting her on the ass. She screamed in glee and pushed my head under the water. I grabbed her and put my hand on her crotch. She tried to knee me gently in the balls but missed. I watched George trudge out of the water toward the others.

"Let's get out," I said to Laura. We walked to the group and dried off in the sun. Even though George was having serious problems, I felt content and happy for a short while. I wasn't having severe mood swings, which I was glad about; the medication I was working very well. I knew a lot of people in recovery who were bipolar as well, but few of them were as stable as I.

"Did that make you feel better?" Laura said to George.

"A little bit, but I'm still tormented," George said. "I'm going home, I think."

"Don't call your wife," Eliot said.

"I won't," George said. "I'm going to sleep for a while; maybe that'll make me feel better."

After he left, we sat quietly for a while. I was thinking how glad I was not to be in his situation. The four of us were in love, and it took the sting out of early recovery.

"What if she insists on a divorce?" Jen said.

"Then he'll just have to go through with it, I think," Eliot said.

"He'll probably lose custody of his kids," Laura said.

"He might not," I said. "Since he's getting clean and taking care of his legal matters, he might be able to see them half the time."

"It's not the same as being married, of course," Eliot said.

"But she's still drinking; maybe the judge would see it his way," Laura said.

"Let's pray it never happens," Len said.

"I feel so badly for him," I said.

"I hope he can stay clean and sober," Laura said. "This could really jeopardize it."

"I'm going back to the house," Eliot said.

"Good idea," I said.

Eliot walked back to the house, and Laura, Jen, and I went to our apartment. The air conditioning felt good, and we were all hungry, so I made a big salad with all kinds of vegetables in it. Then the phone rang.

"Hey, Eliot, what's up?" I answered.

"George isn't here," he said.

A feeling of panic arose in me.

"What are we going to do?" I asked.

"We have to go looking for him," he said.

"I'll pick you up in a few minutes."

I told Jen and Laura to stay put, and I hustled into my car. Two minutes later, I was at the halfway house to pick up Eliot.

"I don't know this town at all. Do you know where to look?" I asked.

"He told me where he used to hang out. I have a pretty good idea where he might be."

The town was small, and soon we were in a very poor section, where all the street people were hanging out. The Mercedes was easily recognizable, so if he were in the area, we would spot him. I had a pit in my stomach. I was worried to death, and I was afraid to cruise around these neighborhoods.

"There it is!" Eliot yelled, as we came up on the car.

George was nowhere to be seen.

"He must be inside," I said. "I'm not going in there."

"I'll go in," Eliot said.

He got out of the car and went into this small, dilapidated house. A few minutes later, he came out with George. Apparently, they had been arguing, because George was still insisting on staying. Eliot was practically manhandling him, and he pushed him toward the car. Finally, George gave in and got in the back seat.

"Why don't you just leave me alone?" George said.

"You're going to get yourself killed!" Eliot said.

I sped away and drove back to their house. George was high as a kite, and I was worried that he'd get kicked out of the halfway house. They didn't drug test every day, but often enough to make it problematic.

"What about my car?" George said.

"We'll pick it up later," Eliot said.

I was worried also about leaving the girls alone, so after I dropped off the guys, I went right back home. Laura and Jen had been very worried, and I told them the story about the rescue. I ate my salad, which I had left there, and the three of us turned on the TV and talked.

## Chapter Nineteen

"What's George going to do if he gets kicked out of the house?" Laura said.

"He can't move back in with his wife; he'll have to go back to his father's, I guess," I said.

"He can probably afford to live on his own," Jen said.

"Maybe he could stay with us for a few days," Laura said.

"Positively not," I said.

"You're his best friend!" Laura said.

"But he's using; anything could happen," I said.

I looked out the window at the ocean and felt my world crumbling about me. I felt that I was under control, but George's escapade had shaken me. Eliot was still strong; he would know what to do. Now George's felonies would bite him in the ass, unless he escaped out of this one. I was thinking of calling Eliot, but decided against it.

"We don't know if he's going to get kicked out anyway," I said.

"Chances are pretty good," Jen said.

"We don't have enough room for a third person," I said. "He probably wouldn't want to stay here as it is."

"His father was very involved in his therapy and recovery," Laura said. "George would probably be more comfortable with him."

"His wife might take him back too," Jen said. "They're fighting now, but she's taken him back before."

I realized how fragile recovery was. Two out of our group had already relapsed; three if I included myself. I knew, somehow, that Eliot wouldn't relapse; he was older and stronger.

"I'm calling Eliot," I said.

"God idea," Laura said.

I waited impatiently for him to answer.

"Hey, how's it going?" I asked.

"I finally got him to sleep," Eliot said.

"When was the last time they tested you?" I asked.

"A few days ago; we're due."

"What are we going to do if he tests positive?" I asked.

"I'm going to give him a sample of my urine," Eliot said.

"Great idea!" I said.

"I only hope we don't get caught," he said.

"How are you going to get caught? They don't watch you do it," I said.

"I know; there's a good chance we'll get away with it."

We talked for a little while longer; then I hung up. I told the women about Eliot's plan, and they were delighted.

"I hope he doesn't go back out today," Laura said. "Now the cravings will have kicked back in, and he'll be right back where he started."

"Eliot will keep a close eye on him," I said. "He probably won't want to use again when he wakes up, but you never know."

"Now I see what a problem I've been," Laura said.

"You haven't been bad," I said.

"I'm going back home," Jen said. "I'll walk."

We gave Jen a kiss goodbye, and I decided to take a bath, which always relieved me when I was stressed. All I could think about was George. When I got out of the bath, I thought about calling Eliot again, but decided to leave him alone. Laura was reading our book, and I felt grateful at least that she seemed in control.

"I'm going to call my father," I said.

"Good idea."

I talked to my father for a long time, and he was always very supportive, like my mother. He never understood, however, not being an alcoholic, what I was going through. I told him I was worried about George, but the only advice he could give me was to leave him alone, which I couldn't do. I told him I loved him, which I rarely did, and he told me he loved me too. After I hung up, I decided to call Eliot.

"What's going on?" I asked.

"He didn't sleep long," Eliot said. "He woke up still high; I'm giving him some coffee."

"I have some sleeping pills you can give him," I said.

"Bring them over."

"See you in a minute."

I told Laura what I was doing and that I'd be back in a minute. I asked her not to leave the apartment. When I got in the car, it wouldn't start. I walked to Eliot's house and found both of them sitting in the kitchen, drinking coffee. George seemed okay.

"Hey, Paulie, what's up?" George said.

"You scared the living shit out of me; that's what's up."

"I know; I'm sorry. It won't happen again," he said.

"I hope not. Did Eliot tell you his plan to get you through the drug test?"

"Yeah, he told me, but I was thinking I might go live with my father."

"Wouldn't it be safer to stay here for a few more months?" Eliot said.

"I don't know if it would be, but maybe you're right,"

George said.

"I think Eliot's got a good point," I said. "Now the cravings will come back, and you won't have any defense against the drugs."

"That's true," he said. "I'm fighting the cravings right now."

I felt really sorry for him, but it was time to toughen up. We would have to keep a close eye on him and drag him to meetings. I gave Eliot the sleeping pills and walked back to the apartment. I was relieved when I found Laura sitting there calmly in front of the television.

"How's George doing?" she said.

"Not very well, but he says he's okay. He's still high, and I think he wants to go back out."

"Jesus, what a mess," she said.

"Eliot will take care of him, but now he says he wants to move out."

"Where's he going to go?"

"With his father, I guess."

"He'll never make it there."

"I know."

"I'd better take care of myself better too," she said.

"Yeah, let me worry about George. You just take care of yourself."

We stayed up for several more hours then went to bed. We made love for an hour. My sensations were so alive, being off the pot, that lovemaking was intense. I fell right to sleep afterwards and slept through the night, which hadn't happened to me since I had gotten sober. In the morning, Laura and I got up early and took a walk on the beach. The sand melted behind us as we made footprints. The past seemed far away, except the last few days. I thought about Linda and knew I had to call her one of these days.

She hadn't called me; I figured she had an idea of what was up. I was happy with Laura now, and I thought things would get better if we stayed sober for a long time.

The sun rose above the hills to the east, and the water started to sparkle. Laura and I both had a lot of energy in the morning.

"Why don't we walk fast and get some exercise?" I suggested. "Jen's been walking every morning since she saw the doctor."

"I'm up for it," she said.

We walked rapidly, and I realized how out of shape I was. My legs were tired after only a few minutes, and I asked Laura to slow down.

"Come on, old man," she said with a laugh.

"I'm going to have to build up a little stamina; I'm only thirty-five," I said laughing.

Laura slowed down, and our walk turned into a leisurely stroll. I was thinking about getting the car fixed; it sounded like the starter, because there was plenty of juice, but it wouldn't turn over. I would have Eliot look at it. I was enjoying our stroll, but was almost afraid to go back to the apartment and get on the phone with Eliot and George. I just wanted peace.

"What are we going to do today?" Laura said.

"Go to the beach, I guess. What else is there to do?"

"We could go shopping."

"We're not going shopping; we hardly have any money, and I'm not going to ask for extra."

"I'm expecting a check tomorrow; I have enough to walk around the stores a little."

"Maybe for an hour or two," I said.

When we got back, there was a message from Eliot. He wanted me to call him. I was worried that something had happened to George.

"Hey, what's up?" I said.

"I wanted to tell you that we got drug tested this morning, and everything went according to plan. George went back to bed, and I think he's through the worst of it. He has a completely different attitude this morning. How's Laura doing?"

"She's fine. Are you going to the beach later? I need you to look at my car."

"Sure, I'll be over in two hours."

"Have you talked to Jen?"

"She seems all right this morning, but she doesn't want to go to the coffee shop for a while," he said.

"Okay, I'll see you later."

I wanted to go to Starbucks but was stuck at home because of the car. There were some stores within walking distance, so I told Laura she could go by herself if she wanted to. I hated feeling responsible for her. I wished she could simply do her own thing, whenever. I decided I couldn't wait for Eliot to look at the car; I called triple A and had it towed to a local shop. They said they could look at it in a few hours.

I called Eliot again, because I was bored and lonely. I knew the pot kept me from those feelings, but now I would have to go through them. It was feelings, above all, that were the most difficult things to handle in sobriety. It occurred to me then, that our philosophers ignored feelings; they were so caught up in thought. My optimism was rooted in feelings as well as thought, a binary that was ignored. Now I wanted only to escape, simply smoke myself into another world.

"Hey, what's up?" Eliot said.

"I'm bored. Why don't you pick me up and we'll go to the coffee shop?"

"Okay, I'll be over in a minute."

I waited impatiently for Eliot to arrive. I sat in front of the television, but couldn't concentrate. I didn't know what to do with myself. Even with Laura gone for a couple of hours, I felt lonely. Eliot arrived a minute later. I told him I had the car towed; he said it sounded like the starter to him too.

"What happens if George wakes up and feels like going out again?" I asked.

"He's on his own. I can't look after him all the time."

We drove to the coffee shop and sat down outside. It was warm, but not too hot, and there was a strong breeze.

"I think George is in real trouble," I said.

"He seemed better this morning, but when the compulsion comes over him, it's really powerful," he said.

"He's caught in a trap. He wants to recover, to save his family and his job, but the pressures of both make him want to go out again," I said.

"If he could only get a few months behind him," Eliot said, "he would be able to handle the pressure a lot better."

"He has to stay in the halfway house, at least for six more months; he's not responsible on his own."

"I'm staying; that's for sure," Eliot said.

"But you're strong, and you've had enough; George obviously hasn't had enough."

The coffee tasted good. I was looking around and noticed some of the other people from the halfway house. It occurred to me there were millions of people throughout the world who were trying to recover. We were a microcosm, and we often felt alone.

"Sometimes we bounce along the bottom for a while, going in and out, until recovery takes hold," Eliot said.

George is really bouncing. Now his car is gone, but he still has his van. That might not last too long either," I said.

"I lost a house, a family, two cars, and a career with the fire department. I hope I'm done," Eliot said.

"It's a good thing you have your pension. You can begin to rebuild."

"You are really lucky. You haven't lost anything," he said.

"I lost myself."

"I know what you mean," he said.

Actually, I had lost a lot, maybe not material things, but I hadn't dated anybody sober. I should have been married at this point, with kids, and a career in teaching, I had done some good painting, but I hadn't touched a novel in five years. I had to rebuild as well.

"We should get back to your house and see what George is up to," I said.

"Good idea."

We drove to the halfway house, and George was gone with the van.

"I'm not going to chase him down this time," Eliot said.

"Let's call his father; he might be over at his house," I said.

We called his father, and sure enough, George was there.

"Thank God you're there; you should have left a note," Eliot told him.

"He'll be back later," Eliot said after he hung up.

Eliot drove me back home, and I was relieved to find Laura listening to music.

"How did the shopping go?" I asked.

"Not very well. That's why I came home early. I didn't have enough money to spend. Everything is so expensive."

"I told you."

"I called Jen; she's doing all right, but she still feels

anxious," she said.

"George is at his father's for the day; Eliot and I panicked. We thought he went back out."

"Let's make love," she said.

"You could have sex ten times a day, couldn't you? I need a nap."

# Chapter Twenty

I slept for an hour, having horrible dreams again. When I woke up, I found Laura lying next to me, naked. She was sleeping. I slowly massaged her ass while she slept. She didn't wake up as I slipped a finger between her legs into her pussy. I got a hard on, then I heard, "What are you doing?"

"I was rubbing you."

"Do you want to fuck?"

"Sure."

We made love for a while then laughed at the ridiculous positions we had tried. We took a shower and fucked again, but this time neither of us came. We decided to go to the beach and called Eliot to see if he wanted to go with us. He said he would call Jen and drag her along with him. It was beautiful out that afternoon. The sun hung high in the sky, and a few puffy white clouds passed by. I brought my notebook with me. I thought it was time to do some writing.

"Do you still really love me?" Laura said.

"Of course. What would prompt you to ask such a question?"

"Oh, we women are insecure, that's all. We need to be told once in a while."

She spread the blanket out in our usual spot, and we waited impatiently for Eliot and Jen to arrive. Finally, I saw them in the distance. They had decided to walk.

"Hey, long time no see," I laughed.

"As much time as we spend together, you would think we'd

get sick of each other," Eliot said.

"We could never sick of you," Laura said.

"Same here," Jen said.

"How do you feel, Jen?" Laura asked.

"Better, I think, but that medicine doesn't seem to work very well."

"You have to give it more time," Eliot said.

"I wonder if they have a medication for a sex addict?" Laura said, laughing.

"You're not a sex addict," I said.

"I could be. Why not? A lot of times we trade one addiction for another. I think I'm a shopaholic too," she said.

"Neither of those will hurt you too much," Eliot said, "unless you spend all your money."

"Why do you think you're a sex addict?" I said seriously.

"I don't know. I want to jump every guy I see," Laura said.

"Well, I want to jump every woman I see too, but that's normal," I said.

"That's not normal," Laura said.

"What's normal anyway?" Jen said.

We laughed for a while and ate some of the food we had brought with us. The wind had died down, and it was getting pretty hot out. I decided to go for a swim, and Laura came with me.

"Do you want to fool around in the water?" she said.

"You are a sex addict. We fucked only a couple of hours ago."

"I told you."

"Let's swim and not fool around. How would that be?" I asked.

"Okay, but I'm warning you; I'm going to jump your bones

later."

"I'll be ready in a few more hours," I said, laughing.

Eliot and Jen came out into the ocean as well, and the four of us stood in the water and talked. Every once in a while, Laura and I splashed each other. Jen seemed a little nervous; I asked her how she felt, but she said she was fine.

"What time did George say he would be back?" I asked Eliot.

"He didn't specify; I guess around dinner time. I'm worried about him, but I can't babysit him."

"Paul keeps an eye on me all the time; I can hardly breathe!" Laura said, splashing me.

"If you hadn't got drunk, I wouldn't be so worried," I said.

"I'm more resolved than ever," Laura said. "I don't mind being tied down, but do you have to use handcuffs?"

"You love it," I said.

"I think I'm getting depressed," Jen said.

"You don't seem too happy," Eliot said.

"Maybe I should take an anti-depressant," Jen said.

"You love your pills, don't you?" Laura said.

"I don't want to get high. I only want to feel normal," Jen said.

"We'll talk to the doctor again," Eliot said.

"I've heard it's very common to get depressed in recovery," I said.

"I feel that way too sometimes," Eliot said.

"I'm glad I'm not the only one," Jen said.

"I know George is very depressed," Laura said.

"We all get depressed from time to time, even normal people have mood swings," I said.

We walked back to the blanket and lay quietly in the sun. Recovery was a bitch, but at least we didn't have to work some stupid job making minimum wage. I was planning on going back to teaching, but I wanted to get my feet planted firmly on earth first.

"Hey, here comes George," I said, as the van pulled up.

"What's up, guys?" he said, as he walked over with a six pack of Pepsi.

"We were talking about you; we're worried to death," I said.

"You don't have to worry about me; I'm fine," he said. "I've decided not to talk to my wife for a while; that should give me a little serenity."

"That's a good idea," Eliot said.

"And I'm going to stay in the halfway house for a few months. I had a long talk with my father, and he set me straight. After I'm out of the house here, I can stay with him. He is the most stable person I know," George said.

"How do you feel?" Laura said. "We're all depressed."

"I feel great. Why are you all depressed?"

"We're not used to being sober this long; we're thinking of getting on anti-depressants," Jen said.

"All of you?"

"Except me," I said. "I tend to run manic; I take the opposite medications."

"Well, I'm not depressed," George said, "and maybe you should all be at a meeting right about now."

"You should talk about meetings. When was the last time you went?" Eliot said.

"I went a few days ago," George said.

"It's suggested that you go every day, and since you just went out again, maybe you should go to two a day for a while," Eliot said.

"Why don't we all go to two a day for a while?" Eliot

suggested.

"Why don't we all go to a meeting?" Jen said.

"I think that's a good idea," Laura said.

"All right by me," Eliot said.

"Then it's decided," I said.

We packed up our things and agreed to meet in an hour; everybody wanted to shower and change. The sun was beginning to set, and we knew there was a meeting at the hall at six o'clock.

Laura and I went home and took a shower together. She wanted to fuck a little, so we did, but it wasn't anything spectacular. I still loved to look at her young, naked body, and I still got hard looking at her. After dressing, we walked to the halfway house and met our friends. We piled into the van and drove to the hall.

"You have to tell them you're coming back after a drink," Eliot said to George.

"I will," George said seriously.

He was going to take some abuse, but that's the way it went. Members of the group were never too happy when someone was coming back. Some were very nice, but others were not. Since he was still in the halfway house, some members would have sympathy, but many would scold him like a child. I had gone through it, and even though it had been difficult, it helped me. Laura had not admitted to coming back; she didn't want to hear it.

"He doesn't have to say anything," Laura said. "He'll only get abused, and it isn't necessary; he knows he fucked up."

"I don't mind," George said. "I could probably use a good lecture. My father didn't say anything."

"He's smart," Laura said. "You were under a great deal of stress; it's perfectly understandable."

"We don't drink, no matter what," Eliot said.

"Fine, have it your way," Laura said.

"Let's not fight," I said. "George can do whatever he wants."

When we arrived at the hall, there were the usual people smoking outside. George and I stood outside with them and had a smoke.

"I'm not going to say I'm coming back," George said.

"That's all right. I understand. Eliot will probably give you a hard time anyway. It's imperative that you not use again; you've got to get it through your head if you can't stop, you're going to lose your wife and kids for sure," I said.

"I know it; that's what scares me the most."

"Don't you want a new start with a clear head and hope for the future?" I asked.

"Of course, I want a new start. Why do you think I'm here?"

"Because you were mandated by the courts; you didn't come in voluntarily."

"I thought you said Eliot would give me a hard time. What do you think you're doing?" George said, hurt by my attack.

"I'm only telling you like it is; you've got to get your act straightened out."

"I'm trying, Paul, I really am."

"All right, forget it now; I'm sorry for giving you a hard time."

I couldn't take back my words though, and I didn't want to. He had to hear the hard truth. Nobody loved him like we did, and nobody understood like we did. The meeting was about to start, so we went inside. George didn't say a word the whole time, and we all left a little disappointed. I had shared how important it was to keep a sense of humor during stressful times, but wondered if I was really doing it myself. We rode home pretty much in silence, and I was feeling uncomfortable. I wanted to be home in Syracuse for the first time in a long time. I picked up my car at the shop, and Laura and I drove home.

"George seemed like he was ready to cry," Laura said.

"Yeah, I was rough on him before the meeting. I shouldn't have said anything."

"Eliot will probably say something to him too," she said.

"I hope he's not cruel," I said.

When we got home, we ate a little something and went right to bed. Laura wanted to make love again, but I declined. The fact that I wouldn't make love all the time kept making her come back for more. I thought about keeping her satisfied in the future, when I was an old man, but couldn't think that far ahead for very long. I slept pretty well that night; we slept well together, which was a blessing. I got up early and made some coffee. The sun was still behind the hills, but the light blue light was beautiful. I liked getting up before Laura and having a bit of time to myself.

I wrote some poetry that morning. I was working on a series about birds, which afforded me a great metaphor.

After an hour or so, Laura got out of bed.

"Good morning," I said.

"Good morning, sweetheart," she said.

"It's going to be another spectacular day," I said.

"You're feeling good," she said, kissing me on the cheek and grabbing my ass.

"Can I read what you've written?" she said.

"Sure."

"Am I your little bird?" she said.

"Yes, darling."

"That is a great poem, honey."

"Thanks. You're the inspiration."

"I know you were worried about writing without pot, but you have no problem."

"It feels a little awkward."

"You'll get used to it," she said.

We were beginning to settle down into a comfortable routine. I had no desire to go back to smoking pot or drinking beer. We communicated well and got along most of the time, though I couldn't wait until we could spend more time alone, separately.

"Have you called Eliot yet?" she asked.

"Not yet."

"He and George are probably at Starbucks already," she said.

"Maybe not; I'll call."

"What's up?" Eliot said.

"Not much. How's George?"

"He seems to be all right."

"Are you guys going to the café?"

"Shortly."

"We'll meet you there. By the way, how's Jen feeling?"

"A little better, but she's still shaky," he said.

Laura and I showered together, but I refused to make love, and she started to pout.

"Cut it out," I said.

"You don't love me."

"Don't be ridiculous."

"Then why won't you?"

"I can't simply make love every time you want to."

"You love the mornings usually."

"Well, not today."

She didn't stop pouting, but I left her alone. I knew she was still immature, and I wished she would hurry up and grow up. We got dressed and drove to Starbucks. I had already had a few cups of coffee, but ordered my usual latte anyway. George, Eliot, and Jen were already sitting outside.

"How are you doing?" I said to Jen.

"I'm seriously thinking about getting on an anti-depressant; I'm going to the doctor's today," she said.

"I'm going with her," Eliot said.

"I'd like to be on some kind of medication too," George said.

"You don't need any," Laura said.

"How do you know?" George said.

"Because the doctor said so; all you need to do is stay off the street drugs," Laura said.

"You're probably right," George said.

"You're not depressed, are you?" Jen asked George.

"Not really, just angry."

"There's always anger management, and the meetings are good for that too," Eliot said.

"I need to get out of my predicament, that's all," George said.

"Stop using and it'll get better," Eliot said.

I talked for a long time, until our little party broke up. I decided to go to a meeting, and Laura said she'd come along. The others went back to the halfway house to see the doctor. George thought he'd see the doctor as well, if only to confirm what the doctor had already said.

The meeting was great; I made everybody laugh, and some of the others made us laugh too. I was starting to branch out with my network, meeting new people and talking to them every day. We had all kinds of people attending the meetings, and sometimes their personalities clashed. Most in our meetings were regular working-class people without much education. It didn't matter to me though. I could relate to anybody. Afterwards, Laura and I went home.

"That was a great meeting," Laura said.

"Yeah, I enjoyed it too."

"I didn't realize you could be so funny."

"When I was growing up, I used to make my whole family laugh. I was funny smoking pot too, but this is better."

"I still feel a little depressed," she said.

"Do you want to see the doctor today too?"

"I think so, but I'm a little wary of taking pills; maybe this will wear off after I am sober a little longer."

"Why don't we see the doc and listen to him; he knows what's going on."

"Okay."

I called the doctor's office and made an appointment for both of us.

"I might be manic-depressive too," Laura said.

"Why do you think that?"

"Sometimes, I have these violent mood swings. One minute I'm perfectly happy; the next minute I'm depressed. That is not normal."

"No, it's not, but it could simply be early sobriety. We'll talk to the doctor."

"You don't really have mood swings any more, do you?"

"I still do, but they're not violent. I'm getting better all the time."

"You take good care of me," she said.

"I love you."

"I love you too," she said. "Let's make love."

"All right."

We fucked our brains out for about an hour and then fell asleep. I had good dreams and woke up two hours later. Laura was already up with coffee, watching TV.

"Why don't you call Eliot and see what the doctor said."

"Good idea," I said.

I called Eliot but didn't get an answer. George was home though.

"What's up?" I said.

"Jen and Eliot are still at the clinic. They should be back soon," George said.

"Why didn't you go?"

"I figured he would say the same thing he said the last time."

"Did you talk to your father today?"

"Yeah, he's coming down for dinner."

"Good, and what about your wife?"

"We've decided to take a break for a while. I still love her, but I'm not sure she's still in love with me."

"I think she loves you, but life is really difficult for her right now," I said.

"It's difficult for both of us, so I think a little distance will do us good."

"That's smart."

"Are you guys going to the beach?"

"Maybe. Do you want to go?"

"Sure. I'll have Eliot call you when he gets back," George said and hung up.

I told Laura what George had said and sat with her in front of the TV. I hated soap operas, but it didn't matter at that moment. Laura knew all the stories and characters, and I thought how nice it would be if she had felt that way about literature. I thought about Linda for a minute, but quickly put her out of my mind. Laura and I had little in common, but we still felt very strongly about each other, and more importantly, we both had a sense of humor.

"Do you want to go to the beach?" I asked her.

"Sure, but my skin is starting to peel. I have to wear some clothes."

"Eliot's going to call in a little while. Let's get ready."

We showered and dressed for the beach. Eliot called and said he would be there with the gang in half an hour. When we arrived at the beach, the three of them were stretched out in the sun.

"We brought some fruit," I said. "Are you guys hungry?"

"I'll have a banana," Eliot said.

"So, what happened with the doctor?" Laura asked.

"He put us on anti-depressants. Jen is taking a little higher dosage than I am," Eliot said.

"How are you feeling, Jen?" I asked.

"Better; I feel more confident now that I'm on medication. My chemistry is all screwed up."

"I'm feeling better too," George said, "now that I don't have to get into a screaming match every day."

"That's good," Laura said.

"How do you guys get along so well?" George asked Laura and me.

"We have our bad moments," I said.

"Yeah, but for the most part, you show each other love and compassion."

"We're still in the early stages; that could change in a couple of years," I said.

"Don't say that," Laura said.

"Let's go for a swim," I said to Laura with a wink.

We went into the ocean and swam out where it was deep.

"Why did you swim out so far? We can't fool around out here," Laura said.

"We'll go back in a minute; I just wanted to swim a little

bit," I said.

I was a strong swimmer and kept going out further. She went back and waited for me. When I got tired, I returned. We were about waist deep, and there were a few people in the water about fifty yards away.

"Do you want to touch me?" she said.

"Of course."

We got on our knees, and the water came up to about our shoulders. I kissed her and put my hand between her legs. I knew exactly how to touch her to make her orgasm.

"Right there," she said.

I rubbed her gently until she same. Then she jerked me off with her hand. At one point, our friends cheered, and we laughed. We walked out of the water exhausted, as if we had swum a mile. The sun was intense, and Laura put her shirt back on. I had no problems at that moment, and I was with my friends; I was at peace.

It didn't take long for that sense of serenity to disappear. I had been thinking about my family back east, and again it popped into my mind. I missed my mother and father, and my brothers. Laura and my friends were not enough, but I didn't want to share this feeling with Laura. I had enough time clean and sober at this point to not be afraid of returning to Syracuse.

"What are you going to do next year?" I asked Eliot.

"I'm going back to school. I want to study to be a counselor, and hopefully, Jen and I will be married," he said.

"What about you, George?" I asked.

"I'm going back to work for my father. That's my best opportunity," George said.

"I'm going back to school too," Jen said.

"What are you going to study?" I asked.

"I should major in pharmacology; I've taken every pill in the book," Jen said, laughing.

"What about you two?" George said.

"I might go back to teaching," I said, "but I don't know; maybe I'll enter a Ph.D. program."

"That would be great, honey," Laura said. "I'm definitely going back to school too, but I don't know for what."

That was one thing that really bothered me about Laura; she had no direction. Linda, on the other hand, had a good idea of what she wanted to do and what interested her. If I applied to a Ph.D. program, it would be at Syracuse University, where I studied before. I knew I wouldn't take Laura with me if I went back to Syracuse. I felt confused again; I had too much time on my hands.

"I think I'm going to go home; I want to do some writing," I said.

"Do I have to go too?" Laura said.

"No, you stay here; I'll see you later."

I walked home, but my real intention was to call Linda, and I wondered if she would be home at this time. It was about dinner time back east, so I thought there would be a good chance of her being home. I called and, fortunately, she answered.

"I'm mad at you," she said.

"I know, I know, and I'm sorry for not calling sooner, but things have been crazy here."

"Well, things have been crazy here too, but that's no excuse for not calling!"

"I'm sorry, but I'm calling now. How have you been?"

"I've been all right. There's been a ton of work, and I have no social life at all. I really miss you."

"I miss you too. I think I'm coming home to Syracuse

shortly."

"When?"

"I don't know; I can't say exactly, but it'll be soon."

"Where are you living now? I called the halfway house, but they say you've moved out."

"I'm living in an apartment near the beach. It's small, but it has a view of the ocean."

"Really! Maybe I should visit you out there. That sounds nice."

"Not yet, honey; I'll come to Syracuse first. I also want to see my mother."

"All right. Anyway, I have to go to a night class, so I'll call you tomorrow."

"Okay, I love you," I said.

"I love you too," she said.

Now my feelings were all stirred up, and I didn't know what to do with myself. I decided to take a shower to clean up after the beach. I knew Laura would be home soon, and I wasn't feeling too comfortable about that. After talking to Linda, I wanted to return to Syracuse very badly. I called my mother and talked to her for a long time. She said she would pay for the plane ticket, and we set a date for a week later. I didn't know how I would break the news to Laura. When Laura got home, I was in the middle of working on a novel.

"Hi, honey," I said.

"Hi. I'm glad you trusted me enough to leave me alone for a while."

"I'm trusting you more and more all the time."

"You seemed in a funny mood earlier. Are you all right?"

"Yeah, I feel better now. Listen, I'm going to Syracuse in a week. My mother really misses me, and she's buying me a ticket."

"That's fine."

"It's all right with you?"

"As long as you don't mind leaving me alone; actually, I think we could use a break. How long are you going for?"

"A week, but if I drive down to see my father, I might stay for a few more days."

"It's all right with me, but I'm not going to sleep very well; I'm used to sleeping with you," she said.

"You'll sleep all right. By the way, we have to go to the doctor in a bit; maybe he can prescribe you some sleep medication?"

"That would be great."

We slept for a while on the couch and then went to see the doctor. We knew him pretty well, and he was glad to see us. He had been a heroin addict himself, so he knew exactly what we were going through. He had been clean for more than twenty years and was a wise old man.

"I'm feeling depressed once in a while," Laura said to him.

He asked her how often she felt depressed and whether she got manic afterwards. They talked for a long time, and then she prescribed her some medicine. Afterwards, Laura said she felt relieved.

"What do you want to do now?" I asked.

"I want to go home and relax," she said.

"I'll cook something," I said.

All I could think about was escaping this situation and going back to Syracuse. I was still in love with Linda, and I was getting bored with Laura. I couldn't handle my new emotions, and I knew all these screwed-up feelings were mostly due to early recovery. We drove home, and I prepared a light meal of salad and chicken breasts. We went to bed early, without making love, and I didn't sleep very well.

# Chapter Twenty-One

Since I had tossed and turned all night, I decided to drag myself out of bed at five o'clock. Laura simply rolled over and went back to sleep; I got up to make coffee. I had experienced some very strange dreams throughout the night and was glad to be awake. I drank several cups of coffee and sat down to write. It suddenly occurred to me that Linda was going to call. I was afraid Laura would pick up the phone. The simple solution was for me to tell her, but I was worried she would have gone to class already, since it was three hours later back east. I called from the balcony, so Laura wouldn't hear me, and Linda was still there.

"Hi, I was going to call you later," she said.

"I have to go out all day, so I thought I'd call you early."

"I was thinking about it, and it sounds like your plans are to stay out in California for a while."

"I haven't really decided, which is why I'm coming back to Syracuse for a while. I've missed some good friends out here, but you know how close I am to my mother."

"Are you still in love with me?"

"Of course. Why do you think I'm coming to see you? I don't expect you to understand what I'm going through, but it involves a great deal of confusion and fear. It's hard for me to explain."

"I'm trying to understand; I really am," she said.

"I love you very much, but I have to work on myself for now; it's not a good idea to be very involved in a relationship."

"Are you breaking up with me?"

"No, of course not. I told you I love you, but I might have to live in California for a while longer. Here I can concentrate completely on my recovery, and my friends mean everything to me."

"How long?"

"It's hard to say; maybe six months to a year."

"A year?"

"I don't know, honey. I might just come back to Syracuse right away; it's hard to tell."

"Well, I don't know what to say, Paul. Call me in a couple of days."

"I will. Bye, sweetheart."

I felt like I was being torn in different directions. I tried to do some writing, but I couldn't concentrate. I decided to go for a walk on the beach. It was so peaceful in the morning; perhaps I could clear my head. There were a few people on the beach, mostly walking their dogs. The sun was beginning to rise, and it was going to be another beautiful day. I thought hard about returning to Syracuse, where the weather was always bad, except in the summer. I had Linda there, and my mother, and brother.

I knew I could make new sober friends in Syracuse, and I could avoid all the old hangouts. The only thing was that as soon as I got to Syracuse, I would want to be in California again. I was uncomfortable wherever I was, and I knew it would be the same in Syracuse. I walked and walked, and sure enough, my thoughts began to slow down. When I got back to the apartment, I found Laura sitting leisurely, listening to the stereo and drinking coffee.

"Where have you been?" she asked.

"Walking on the beach."

"I figured. How do you feel?"

"Better now."

"How did you sleep?"

"Not very well. I had a lot of weird dreams. How about you?"

"I slept well; I'm sorry you had a rough night."

"I'm all right now."

"How was the beach?"

"Spectacular! I was thinking maybe we should get a dog. It would be nice to have one around."

"Or maybe have a baby," she said.

"Let's try the dog first," I said.

"Oh, come on, Paul, a baby would bring us closer together."

"Or pull us apart. I'm not ready to have a baby. We're not even married yet."

"I stopped taking the pill."

"What? Why? You can't do that without consulting me. Are you trying to trap me?"

"I just thought it would be nice to get pregnant; I was afraid to ask you. I'm not trying to trap you; we're planning on getting married anyway."

"Well, we're not having sex until you go on the pill again. I'm not ready for a baby. What, are you out of your mind?"

The finality and reality of being married had hit me. I was not ready for this at all. I wanted to call Eliot or my mother. I didn't know which, so I picked Eliot. I had to cool off; I didn't want to argue with Laura.

"Hey, what's up?" Eliot said.

"Laura went off the pill, and I'm a mess."

"Is she pregnant?"

"We don't know yet."

"Go to the drugstore and get a pregnancy test."

"Good idea; I'll talk to you later."

Why was it that I couldn't think of these things myself? I told Laura I would be right back and drove to the store. All I could think was that she was pregnant, and my plans with Linda would be ruined. Of course, I didn't have any set plans with Linda, but that's how I was thinking. When I got back, Laura tested herself, and the test came out negative.

"What a relief!" I said.

"I don't see what's wrong with having a baby. We're in love and planning on getting married," she said.

"The marriage is off; I'm very upset," I said.

"What?"

"You heard me! I'm fucking pissed off!"

She didn't say anything for a while. I had finally said what I had been thinking for a long time. I knew that marrying Laura wasn't right. I was still in love with Linda, and I wanted to be back in Syracuse. Here was my excuse to escape. Finally, she said something.

"I hate you!"

"Well, right now, I hate you too."

"I'll get back on the pill; I don't see why the marriage has to be off."

"I don't see how it's going to work out if I can't trust you."

"You can trust me, and I don't really hate you; I know it's my fault."

"I don't hate you either, and I knew you want to hold on to me, but this isn't the way to do it."

"I know; you're right. I won't pull a stunt like that again."

"Good! Enough said."

I was still angry, of course, but she had helped me put things into perspective. I knew I could trust Linda, and I was more determined than ever to return to Syracuse. I could stay at my own house, perhaps live with Linda, and start a new life again. I knew I would break Laura's heart, and it would hurt me too, but she was young; she'd get over it.

"Do you want to go to the beach? It'll make me feel better," I said.

"That's a good idea. I'll shower."

She took her clothes off in front of me, and I wanted to fuck her right on the spot. She showered, and I called Eliot to tell him to meet us at the beach.

"Is she pregnant?" he asked.

"No, thank god."

"Good! We'll see you in an hour."

I got in the shower with Laura and started sucking on her tits. Her tanned legs stretched all the way up to her neck, and I buried my face in her crotch. I figured I could fuck her, as long as I didn't come inside her. She sucked on my cock and made me come. She swallowed it all and smiled at me afterwards.

"Now that's the way to get up in the morning," I said.

"Have you forgiven me?" she said.

"I can't stay mad at you," I said.

"Same with me," she said, smiling.

"Let's go to the beach," I said.

"Great idea."

We dressed and walked to our spot. I didn't know if George or Jen would show up, but I thought they probably would. I had that great afterglow following good sex. My thoughts drifted to Syracuse, and the wet spring they were having. I missed the anticipation of spring in California. We spread our blankets on the sand and stretched out under the sun. We both wore t-shirts, not wanting to get burned.

"Are we still going to get married?" Laura asked.

"We'll see."

"You're not going to hold a grudge, are you?"

"No, I don't think so, but I'm having second thoughts."

"Why?"

"Because I can't trust you. That's why."

"Fine."

We didn't speak to each other again until Eliot and Jen arrived.

"How are you guys doing?" Eliot said.

"Just great!" Laura said.

"What's the matter?" Jen said.

"Paul doesn't want to get married now," Laura said.

"Why not, Paul?" Jen said.

"She went off the pill without telling me," I said.

"Why did you do that, sweetheart?" Jen said to Laura.

"I want to get pregnant!" Laura said.

"That's not the way to do it," Eliot said.

"Thank you," I said.

"You'll get over it, Paul," Jen said.

"I can't trust her; that's the point," I said.

"I told you I was sorry; I won't do it again," Laura said.

"You're not pregnant, are you?" Jen asked.

"No," Laura said.

"Good! Then the trust can be rebuilt," Jen said.

I was getting angry all over again. I thought that Linda would have never pulled a stunt like that. I wished that Jen would stay out of it. I didn't like her taking sides. Eliot kept his mouth shut for the most part, and I knew he understood how I felt. I decided to go back to the apartment to cool off.

"I'll see you guys later," I said.

"Don't leave, Paul," Jen said.

"Mind your own business," I snapped. "I'm sorry," I said, right away.

"That's all right," she said. "I know you're angry."

I went back to the apartment and tried calling Linda, but she wasn't home. I didn't know what to do with myself; I was still angry. I called George and he was home.

"Hey, what's up?" he said.

"Did Eliot tell you that Laura went off the pill?"

"Yeah, he told me."

"I'm glad I'm going back to Syracuse in a few days; I need some time off."

"It'll be good to see your family," he said.

"Listen, I don't feel like talking right now. I only wanted to check in with you," I said.

"Okay, pal; I'll see you later."

After I got off the phone, I decided to take a shower. It felt good to be under the water. Then, I took a nap. I had a strange dream about Linda finding out about Laura and woke up with a start.

## Chapter Twenty-Two

"What the fuck!" I said to myself.

I was still angry. I called Linda again and left a message. I hadn't felt so bad in a long time, and I thought about finding some pot and escaping. I decided to go back to the beach instead and face my feelings. They were all stretched out, relaxing, when I returned, and I got a warm welcome.

"Feel better?" Eliot said.

"A little," I said.

"I'm so sorry," Laura said, giving me small kisses all over my face.

"It's all right, honey," I said.

"I'm sorry too," Jen said. "I shouldn't meddle in your business."

"It's all right, really," I said. "Don't worry about it."

"Have you talked to your mom today?" Eliot said. "She must be looking forward to seeing you."

"No, I'm going to call her later."

"You seem still upset," Laura said.

"I am a little, I guess," I said.

"You should be flattered that I want to have a child with you," Laura said.

"I am, but I'm not crazy about the methods."

"You're right; I don't know what I was thinking, but I knew you would say no, so I tried to trick you. I'm so sorry."

"I'll try to understand, but let's drop the subject now," I said.

"I've moved up the date to go to Syracuse. I'm leaving tomorrow."

"Okay," Laura said sullenly.

"We're going to miss you," Jen said.

"And you'd better come back," Eliot said.

"I'll be back soon, I promise; I'll miss you guys," I said.

In the back of my mind, I was thinking that I might return to Syracuse for good. I lay on the beach next to Laura and closed my eyes. I envisioned making love to Linda, and I missed the way she kissed. I had lost something with Laura. I didn't know if it was respect or patience, but it just wasn't the same. My anger turned to sadness, and a certain loneliness that I couldn't describe.

"Let's go get an ice cream," I said to Laura.

"Okay."

We walked, hand in hand, down the beach. I knew that I didn't love her any more, and I thought back to what one of the counselors had said about rehab love: "It won't last."

I was anxious for the day to be over with, so I could wake up in the morning refreshed and looking forward to my trip home.

"Are you really coming back?" Laura said.

"Yes, of course."

"Will you call me as soon as you arrive?"

"Sure."

She could sense that my feelings had changed; I could tell by her tone. We got an ice cream and sat on the beach by ourselves.

"You're not coming back, are you?" she said.

"I'm coming back; don't worry."

"You hate me now."

"Nonsense."

"I don't want you to go."

"I have to."

"Take me with you; I'd love to meet your mother."

"I can't."

I was feeling very sad. I thought this might be the last night that I would spend with her. When I looked at her, she was crying.

I held her tightly and whispered, "I still love you."

"No, you don't."

I let it go at that; I wasn't going to continue lying to her. She knew the passion was gone, and we were both in tears.

"Let's go home," she said. "I want to fuck you for the last time."

"It won't be the last time."

"Come on," she said, grabbing my hand.

We walked home and took a shower together. I wanted to make love to her, but I couldn't get hard.

"I'm sorry, honey," I said.

"I'm sorry too."

She was silent for a long time, and I sat in front of the television, imagining my trip back home. I thought that I loved Linda more than ever and wanted to sit with her, helping to work on one of her papers.

"Let's go out to dinner," Laura finally said.

"That's fine with me."

We went to dinner at a small Italian place nearby and ate in silence. All I could think about was returning to Syracuse. I could tell Laura was sad and angry. We went home and got to bed early. I had to drive to Los Angeles and catch my plane in the morning. I had crazy dreams that night, full of fear and anxiety.

At five a.m., I dragged my ass out of bed and took a shower.

Laura was still sleeping when I made the coffee. I was sad and excited at the same time. I thought about so many people that I knew in Syracuse, and I thought about my friends in California.

I told Laura it was time to get up, and she reluctantly got out of bed. She drove me to the airport and said goodbye quickly. I could tell she was holding back her tears. I kissed her and told her I would be back soon. I got on the plane and felt that I was a free man.

I wanted to go to Syracuse, but when I got to Chicago, I had a change of heart. I missed Laura and thought that I was throwing away a great relationship. In Chicago, I got a plane ticket back to L.A. I knew I was crazy, but that didn't stop me from wanting to be with Laura. I had begun a new life in California, and I wanted to continue it. Going back to my old life in Syracuse was distasteful to me, and I knew that Linda wasn't right for me. When I got to L.A., I took a shuttle to Ventura, and took a cab to our apartment. I knocked on the door and cried when I saw Laura's face. She was so surprised and overjoyed to see me that she grabbed me and squeezed me as tightly as she could.

"Will you marry me?" I asked.

"Those are the most wonderful words I have ever heard," she said.

Printed in the USA
CPSIA information can be obtained
at www.ICGtesting.com
JSHW021408220923
48800JS00001B/72